MONTANA MAVERICKS

Welcome to Big Sky Country! Where spirited men and women discover love on the range.

HIDDEN GEMS RANCH

As the seasons change in the small town of Tenacity, Montana, so does opportunity. The high school football team has a shot at a winning season, and with fall pumpkin festivals, Christmas events and the discovery of precious kimberlite, the town is buzzing. For some cowboys and cowgirls, though, the prize they most value seems just out of reach. Could love be the ultimate gem discovered in Tenacity?

THE MAVERICK'S LEGACY

Rancher Jesse Abernathy is baffled why a beautiful rodeo star like Carly Hawkins would be interested in him, a simple widower with family obligations. Carly has worked hard for her success, and she honestly isn't sure what the future holds. She only knows how Jesse makes her feel right now, and she doesn't want to give that feeling up...

Dear Reader,

Have you ever had a dream, but you're not sure if you should risk everything for it? Carly Hawkins knows that feeling well. After a turbulent childhood, she's gained more financial security than she ever imagined from being part of the world-famous Hawkins Sisters.

But after a public breakup, Carly wants a fresh start. She purchases a homestead in Tenacity to start her dream project—a riding school for foster kids. When she meets Jesse Abernathy, she wonders if love might be in the cards, as well. But when the rodeo life tempts her back, Carly faces a hard choice: continue with the only life she's known, or risk everything to follow her heart and build something new.

This choice is the heart of Carly's story, and it resonates with me because it's a pivotal moment that many of us encounter.

It was an honor to write Carly and Jesse's story, and I hope you enjoy it. For more about my books, you can visit my website, kellistorm.com, where you can also subscribe to my newsletter.

Kelli Storm

THE MAVERICK'S LEGACY

KELLI STORM

Harlequin

MONTANA MAVERICKS

Special thanks and acknowledgment are given to Kelli Storm for her contribution to the Montana Mavericks: Hidden Gems Ranch miniseries.

Harlequin® MONTANA MAVERICKS

MIX
Paper | Supporting responsible forestry
FSC® C021394
www.fsc.org

Recycling programs for this product may not exist in your area.

ISBN-13: 978-1-335-14363-1

The Maverick's Legacy

For questions and comments about the quality of this book, please contact us at CustomerService@Harlequin.com.

Harlequin Enterprises ULC
22 Adelaide St. West, 41st Floor
Toronto, Ontario M5H 4E3, Canada
www.Harlequin.com

HarperCollins Publishers
Macken House, 39/40 Mayor Street Upper,
Dublin 1, D01 C9W8, Ireland
www.HarperCollins.com

Printed in Lithuania

1 2 3 4 5 6 7 8 9 10 LIT 28 27 26 25

Kelli Storm earned her bachelor's degree from Grand Valley State University and is the author of the Challenge Accepted series for Harlequin Special Edition. She also wrote the young adult fantasy series The Assembly Hearts, which includes *Desolate*. Kelli's debut adult romance, *His Small-Town Challenge* (Harlequin Special Edition, 2025), is an ode to her love of boy bands. She lives in the Great Lake State with three rescue dogs and a fifteen-year-old fish named Henry O'Malley.

Books by Kelli Storm

Montana Mavericks: Hidden Gems Ranch

The Maverick's Legacy

Harlequin Special Edition

Challenge Accepted

The Wedding Promise
First Comes Marriage
The Fake Dating Dare
His Small-Town Challenge

Visit the Author Profile page at Harlequin.com.

To all the women who took the leap
and followed their dreams

Chapter One

Carly Hawkins stared at the large ranch home, wondering for the hundredth time what on earth she'd been thinking when she'd bought it.

No. She knew exactly what she'd been thinking. She had stopped by her sister Amy's house to see her almost year-old niece and had been hit with...*feelings*.

As she'd watched her sister cuddle baby Josephine, something foreign had slammed into her. An idea that maybe life had more to offer her other than the rodeo circuit.

The truth was she was getting tired—exhausted from the nonstop grind of performing. When she'd first started her career, she'd been obsessed with becoming as successful as possible. Her fear of failure stemmed from a turbulent childhood in the foster system, spending many years with nothing but the secondhand clothes on her back to call her own.

And for the most part she'd met the goals she'd set for herself.

Her family were world-famous rodeo stars. She and her sister Elizabeth had toured Australia for years. That was before the tragic loss of Elizabeth's husband. Her sister had decided she needed a fresh start, so she'd moved herself and her twins back to the States. Carly had missed them like crazy after they'd left. A part of her thought Elizabeth would return, but she eventually met a widower and got a second chance at happiness.

Carly was overjoyed for her. If anyone deserved to find love again, it was Elizabeth. But that left one single person in the family. Carly. Which…she was fine with.

She had more important things to worry about than a husband and babies.

Like becoming the biggest rodeo star in the world.

At least that had been her dream. Because in the back of her mind, there was always the lingering fear that everything could be taken away again. She had enough money now that, if she was careful, she never had to work again. She could walk away from her current life if she wanted to.

After discovering her boyfriend, Fletch, had been cheating, and enduring the media storm their breakup had caused in Australia, Carly knew she needed a change. The injury she'd suffered in Perth had already shaken her, and this was the final push. She flew to Montana to spend time with family, stopping first in Bronco for a period before heading to Tenacity to see her sister Amy. On the way, she spotted a For Sale sign, and before she knew it, she'd bought herself a house.

Speaking of family…

A truck pulled down her long gravel driveway. Carly's wayward thoughts were instantly muffled as she recognized her parents' vehicle, pulling a horse trailer. Her beloved horse, Nieve, let out a loud neigh that could be heard over the crunch of the tires.

"Hello, darlin'," her dad called out as he pulled the

truck close to where she stood. "Where do you want me to put your baby?"

"I have a stall all ready for him," Carly replied, waving at the barn a short distance away. As her mom got out of the vehicle, Carly moved to the side of the trailer to check her horse over.

Nieve was a true beauty, with a shimmering white coat and soft pink nose. They'd been all over the world together. It had been painful for Carly to be away from him, but she'd had to keep the horse at her parents' while she'd gotten her things moved into the ranch.

Carly reached up to touch him through the open window of the trailer. "Hey, my sweet boy."

The horse bumped his nose against Carly's palm in response, letting out a soft snort of air. She smiled in response, her heart overflowing with love for the stallion.

As soon as she was brought into Suzie and Arthur's home, an angry foster kid at eight years old, they'd thrown her onto a horse to work out her issues. And it worked for the most part. For the first time in her young life, she'd felt safe openly loving another sentient being. She'd poured herself into caring for each horse her parents owned. Though she loved and appreciated every one of them she worked with, there was something magical about her bond with Nieve.

"We'll go for a ride soon, okay?" she promised him, and he gave her that look that assured her he understood and he'd keep her to it.

"He was as good as gold," her mom said as she walked over to them. "Considering he hates everyone but you and his fans."

Carly laughed as she stepped back from the trailer.

She tapped the side of her dad's truck, and he continued toward the barn.

Her mom hugged her tight once the vehicle was a safe distance away. "It's so good to have you home, honey."

Carly pulled back, taking in her mom's peach-colored complexion, her soft blue eyes, and her ash-blond hair that was more silvery than Carly remembered.

"You act like I've been gone forever." Carly grinned. "I've been back several times in the past few years, what with Elizabeth marrying Jake and Amy having Josephine."

"But that was just a quick stop, a few days here and there. Now you're home and I'll get to see you all the time."

She gave her mom an amused look. "You live in Bronco. That's not exactly around the corner."

Suzie waved that away dismissively. "Yes, but it's a much easier drive to get to you than flying halfway across the world."

"You and Dad are the ones who introduced us to this life," Carly reminded her. Her father had once had a successful career in rodeo riding himself until he'd busted his knee during one freak fall.

"And don't think I haven't had my moments of regret," her mom replied. "But now I have all my girls within an hour and a half's drive of each other."

"Yeah," Carly said, turning to look at her house once more. It really was a gorgeous homestead. From the front of the house, it looked like a single-story ranch. Large stones made up the base while the rest of it was covered in thick, dark wood boards. But the home was deceptively bigger than it looked with a lower walkout basement that overlooked the mountains in the distance and woods that ran along the property.

"Uh-oh," her mom muttered.

Carly looked at her, her eyebrows pulled together. "What?"

"I know that look."

Carly crossed her arms across her chest. "What look? I have no look."

"Are you regretting moving back?" her mom asked.

"No, not really," she answered. "It's just going to take some getting used to. Not being on the road. It's all I've known for years."

"Well." Suzie wrapped an arm around Carly's waist as they both looked at the house. "At least you bought a beautiful piece of property with a gorgeous view. Tenacity is booming. Hold on to this land for a while, and you'll likely double your investment, if not more so."

Her dad drove back to them, towing the now empty trailer. Arthur got out of the truck and wrapped Carly in a bear hug. The man was still the size of a grizzly despite getting on in age. Ranch work kept him young. While his skin barely had a wrinkle in it despite the amount of hours he spent under the sun, his hair was starting to gray at the sides. To her, though, he'd always be that quiet hero who'd shaken her hand solemnly the first time they'd met and promised her that as long as he was breathing, nothing would ever hurt her again. He'd kept his word over the years too. She could never repay either of her parents for the love and support they'd given her since they'd taken her in. She owed them everything.

"You got yourself some nice land, Carly-bear," her dad said after he finished hugging her.

"That's what we were just talking about," Suzie said, looking at Arthur with the same sweet warmth that she always did when she looked at her husband.

"What are your plans for that area?" he asked, pointing to an empty expanse of cement to the left of the barn.

"I'm not sure yet," Carly said. "Why?"

"Nothing really," he replied. "I seem to recall when you were little that you said you wanted to someday run a horse-riding school for kids in the foster system. That'd be a real nice spot to build an office."

"Oh, yeah. That was the dream, wasn't it?" Carly said.

When her parents introduced her to horse riding when she was a child, it had been so natural to her. She would think about the few friends she'd made in the system who were missing out on the exhilarating freedom of riding a thousand-pound animal at top speed. They'd never get to enjoy the feeling of being so out of control and in control at the same time, and it saddened her. She remembered vowing after she won her first championship that she'd someday start a riding school so that kids in the system could have the same experience.

Carly pushed the thought aside before the little seed her dad had just planted could grow any further. "I don't want to plan anything right now. I haven't taken a vacation in years. All I have in my immediate future is a well-earned break. Especially after everything that happened with Fletch."

"Never did like that man," her dad grumbled. "He was too smarmy."

"I know, Dad. You've told me that at least a hundred times."

It never bothered her much that her family hadn't liked

her boyfriend of two years, which should have told her something. She and the attractive Aussie had been the it couple of the rodeo circuit, appearing in magazines across Australia. Sponsors couldn't get enough of them.

She'd dated Fletch because he was fun to be around. He'd dated *her* because being in a relationship with one of the Hawkins Sisters gave him the credibility that his daddy's money couldn't—despite his father owning the Australian Circuit she'd traveled in. Together they were elevated to the international spotlight, and he'd loved it.

Carly hadn't felt too heartsick the day she'd caught him cheating. Was she humiliated? Yes. There had been a huge scandal. It was one of the reasons she'd decided to come back to the States when she did. But did she care otherwise? Not really. That should have been the biggest red flag to her that she wasn't in love with the man. If she'd stayed, they would have broken up eventually anyway.

She wasn't sure if she'd ever truly been in love before. She'd been too focused on her career. She wondered sometimes if it would ever happen for her like it had her sisters. Until it did, Carly wanted to focus on her next steps if she ended up taking an indefinite break from the rodeo circuit.

"Anyway," she said, changing the subject. "The house might just end up being a stopping point for me. A place I can stay in between tours. There's no point in starting a business when I can't maintain it."

Her mom side-eyed her. "It's something to think about. There are more options than rodeo out there."

"What's wrong with rodeo?" Carly asked, her stubbornness rising.

"You said yourself that you've grown tired of the constant traveling," her mom replied. "Especially after your injury."

Carly winced at the memory. A friend in Australia had asked her to take some photos on top of their horse. They'd wanted some publicity for their new breeding stables. Carly hadn't realized that the horse had a fear of snakes, and she'd been distracted by the paparazzi nearby shouting at her about Fletch. When a snake had slithered in front of the racehorse, the poor animal had startled. Carly had done her best to control the situation, but she'd ended up with a couple of cracked ribs when the horse threw her. She'd been lucky not to get injured any worse. Thankfully she was already feeling better, other than the occasional twinge of pain.

Her mom continued, "I think you should consider all your options. The world is your oyster, you know. Maybe take Nieve for a ride around the property and enjoy your new home. A good ride always puts things in perspective."

Carly nodded, and after a short visit, her parents headed back to Bronco. Deciding to take her mother's advice, Carly headed toward the stables.

As she walked, she couldn't help but think about what her father said. She had plenty of room to build a riding school that could help kids in the system. It would take a lot of work. She needed to rebuild several of the stables in the barn and repair the paddock. She'd need to build an office to conduct business and have a public bathroom for her students and their foster parents. There was room for outdoor classes, but she'd want to make sure they had a working indoor arena for bad weather. She could already picture it in her head.

Stop that! You're supposed to be relaxing. Not planning more work.

Well...she'd never been one to relax and sit still anyway. Her endless energy was what used to get her in trouble in foster homes before Suzie and Arthur took her in. But she didn't like to think about back then.

It wouldn't hurt for Carly to get some numbers together and make some calls. Maybe she could even look into ways to rescue horses bound for the slaughterhouse.

Nieve greeted her with a rambunctious whinny when she entered the barn. He was as anxious as Carly to get out and go for a ride. Riding always cleared both of their heads.

"Yeah," she said, rubbing between his eyes. "Let's get out of here."

A short time later, they were slowly sauntering through the trails behind her house. She breathed in the fresh pine scent of the woods, watching with amusement as a squirrel chattered at her from the tree above before scurrying into its nest.

"I know," she murmured. "I'm on your turf."

Her earlier concerns about the direction of her life seemed to vanish as they continued down the trail, passing through a shallow creek. As much she loved Australia, there was nothing quite like the forest greenery of the States. She'd been all over the world now. Nothing quite compared.

As she stared at the canopy of leaves above her, she felt Nieve tense underneath her legs. Carly glanced down at the horse, noticing the snowy beauty's ears had shot straight.

Carly reached down slowly for the bag attached to her

saddle where she always kept bear spray for any predators that might try to creep up on her.

A twig snapped to her left, and she swirled in that direction.

Only to come face to face with the most gorgeous man she had ever seen.

Chapter Two

Jesse Abernathy stared at the woman in front of him, completely dumbstruck. He hadn't expected to meet anyone on the trails in this part of Tenacity, considering they were a part of his brother Grayson's property. It was why he'd told his son that it was a great spot to get some peace and quiet.

They'd both needed it after the craziness of his brother's home, where they were temporarily staying. Jesse thought the world of Grayson's girlfriend and her daughters. But between the three girls; Grayson's son, Adam; and their four dogs it was *a lot* to get used to, especially after it had been just Oscar and him for so long.

He figured he and his son could both use some time out in nature. It was a beautiful day for September. The weather wasn't too hot or cold. The sky above was bright blue and clear of clouds. The woods smelled like wet dirt and fresh pine needles. The birds were singing loud from the branches above, their songs not muffled by the sound of cars and buses going down the street like they were in Houston. Everywhere he looked there was greenery instead of cement, and it relaxed him in ways he hadn't experienced in years. It was one of the reasons he moved them to Tenacity—to get his son out in the fresh air.

He'd always made sure Oscar knew how to ride a horse, even though they'd spent of majority of their lives living in the city. Being on a horse was a part of an Abernathy's DNA. Riding was as natural to Oscar as breathing. As an autistic kid, there were many things he struggled with in life, but being around horses wasn't one of them. It was a relief to Jesse and something that the two could bond over. He and Oscar would go riding a couple of times a month while they'd lived in Houston. It was a refreshing change that they could now ride whenever they wanted.

The problem was that his plan hadn't worked out so well—yet. Between Jesse working almost nonstop on building their new home and Oscar recently starting at a new school, they really hadn't had time to go riding. But after JenniLynn's youngest had the mother of all tantrums that morning, he figured he and Oscar could both use a change of scene for the day.

Jesse never expected to run into Eva Mendes's lookalike or prettier twin. The woman wore a pink Western-style top and tight jeans with the ankles covered by expensive-looking cowgirl boots. Her long brown hair was pulled into a loose ponytail half hidden under a Stetson hat. Even from a distance, he could tell she had the features of an angel with sharp cheekbones and rich coffee-brown eyes.

"Ma'am," he finally said, tipping his own hat at her as the cream-colored mare under him shifted her feet.

"You're on my property," she said in a tight voice. Her hand hovered over her saddle bag in a way that made him nervous. What was she hiding in there? Pepper spray? Something worse? Even her horse looked at him like he was a criminal.

Jesse frowned, his calm replaced with sudden tension. Had they gone too far and wandered onto someone else's land? He could hear the sound of water rumbling to his right, which meant that they hadn't passed Crystal Creek yet.

Oscar came up behind him on his borrowed Paint, and the woman's eyes flitted from him to the teenager next to him. She relaxed at the sight of his son, her grip loosening its hold on the bag attached to the saddle.

Jesse realized what must have been going through her head, running into a stranger—a man, no less—in the middle of the woods when she least expected it. His hands flew up, trying to assure her he meant her no harm. He nodded toward Oscar.

"This is my son," Jesse said, trying to give her further reassurance. Not that it wasn't obvious. With the exception of his green eyes, which Oscar had gotten from his mother, he was Jesse's miniature.

"Oh! Hello," she said, her face lighting. A gentle smile formed on her lips. The shift in her features startled him. Had he called her pretty earlier? It was such a weak word to describe the woman in front of him. She was stunning.

She was… God, he found her attractive. Jesse couldn't remember the last time he'd been attracted to someone. He didn't count sex. Sex was easy. This woman made him ache to get her comfortable, to trust him. He bit back the urge to ask her on a date. He couldn't even remember the last time he'd dated someone. It had been years.

Hell, he didn't know the woman's name and he was already thinking about asking her out. What kind of magic was she weaving over him? Not that she'd automatically accept. There was an extremely good chance she already had a man in her life. There was no way she was single.

On the off chance she was available, given the fact that she'd just been about to pepper spray him—he'd bet his new cabin on it—he very much doubted she'd accept a date with him.

Not that he could get involved with someone right now, so he needed to pull himself together. Because the only thing he should be focused on was his son and how he was adjusting to life in Tenacity.

Oscar didn't say anything in return to the woman's greeting, which wasn't unusual, given how shut down he'd become lately.

The woman turned her attention back to Jesse and lifted a perfectly shaped eyebrow. Right. There was the matter of her thinking he'd trespassed.

"There seems to be a misunderstanding here. This is Abernathy property," he said. When she opened her mouth looking ready to argue, he hurried, "Anything east of this creek is now Grayson Abernathy's ranch, the Ambling Hills."

"I…" the woman started to say before her face turned a fascinating shade of pink. "Well…this is embarrassing. I do seem to remember crossing a creek on my ride, come to think of it." She gave him a sheepish grimace. "I was lost in thought and not paying attention to my surroundings. I'm sorry for my rudeness."

"Not to worry. I didn't take anything you said as being rude. It's better to be safe than sorry these days," he said, giving her saddle bag a knowing nod. He wondered again what she kept in there.

She gave him a weak smile. It looked like she was about to turn her horse around, but he really didn't want her to leave just yet. He was enjoying this strange encounter. "I'm Jesse Abernathy, by the way. And this is Oscar."

"Nice to meet you both." She gave Oscar another sweet smile. "I'm Carly. Carly Hawkins."

Oscar suddenly perked up straight. "Carly Hawkins?"

Jesse looked between his son and Carly, his eyebrows pulling together. Oscar rarely got excited about anyone or anything other than sports. While he was happy to see a little animation on his son's face, Jesse felt like he was missing something here.

Carly seemed unfazed by Oscar's reaction. "That's right. And this is Nieve."

She patted the gorgeous white horse's neck who *still* seemed to be looking at Jesse judgmentally.

"You're one of the Hawkins Sisters!" Oscar shouted, startling everyone.

"Whoa," Jesse murmured to his horse as it moved sideways at the noise. "Oscar, remember what I told you. We can't shout around the horses."

"Sorry," he told his dad, completely unfazed, even as he had to settle his own horse. He looked back at Carly. "But you *are* a Hawkins Sister, right?"

"I am that," she confirmed.

"Dad," Oscar said, giving his father an eager look that hit Jesse right in the center of his heart. He was used to Oscar's encyclopedic knowledge of football stats, but Jesse was happy to see his son so interested in something other than football. Oscar continued, "This is Carly Hawkins. She's set multiple National Finals Rodeo records, won three world championships, and Nieve won Horse of the Year three years in a row for barrel racing."

"Is that right?" Jesse said, giving the horse a doubtful

look. The beast tossed its mane and turned its head away as though it was already bored with him.

"And Carly has four sisters—Tori, Amy, Faith, and Elizabeth," Oscar explained to his dad before turning back to Carly. "You and your sister toured Australia for years. You won the Ariat National Finals Rodeo a couple of years ago before your injury—"

"Injury?" Jesse asked. His mind raced with a million different meanings for the word *injury* in the span of a second before landing on the one he hated thinking about the most.

His mind flashed to the night that destroyed his life…

Love, hang on. Help is on the way. Don't you leave me, dammit! Stay with me, MaryBeth. I need you. We need you.

"It was nothing," Carly said, waving the injury away. "A couple of cracked ribs. It wasn't anything that I haven't had to deal with before." She looked over at Oscar. "I'm impressed that you know so much."

Oscar gave her a bashful grin. "I love sports. All sports."

Jesse barely heard them. He was too busy fighting back the nausea rising in his throat. He could very clearly imagine Carly's injury. In the blink of an eye, he saw her lying lifeless on the ground. He'd gone through something similar before. That horrific moment when he'd found his wife unconscious on the floor of their kitchen. He'd been too late to save her from the brain aneurysm that stole her from them. Nearly ten years later, he still had nightmares about that day.

"Are you okay?" Carly asked.

"What?" he said in a daze. He was going to be sick.

"You went a little pale."

He forced himself to look at Carly, taking in the concern on her face. She was okay. She was right there in front of him, unlike MaryBeth. He gave himself a little shake of the head to snap out of it.

"I'm fine. I…" Jesse looked back at Oscar. "We should probably get going. I told your uncle we'd be back in time for dinner."

"Are you in town visiting?" Carly asked.

"We moved here last month," Oscar answered. "We're staying at my Uncle Grayson's for now, but Dad is building us our own cabin. We're going to be ranchers."

Carly tilted her head. "In Tenacity?"

Jesse stumbled his way back to the present, trying not to reveal how shaken he felt. "That's right. Over on Ambling Hills."

His brother had been kind enough to give Jesse and Oscar part of his land. It was enough to start up his own functioning ranch. The house they were building was more of a glorified cabin, but it was their own place under the Montana sky. It was all he wanted for his son.

Carly's lips tilted up, the movement immediately drawing Jesse's eyes. It erased some of the earlier horror he'd felt at the idea of her being injured, which was an extreme reaction to have over someone who was a stranger.

"I guess that makes us neighbors," she said, completely unaware of the turmoil that Jesse was experiencing.

But that finally got his attention. His brows shot to his hairline. "You live in Tenacity?"

"I just moved here actually. I bought the property next door. And speaking of, I should probably get off your family's land."

"It's no problem," Jesse replied quickly. "You're welcome here anytime."

Carly's uptilted lips bloomed into a full smile. Jesse had to force his eyes away so she wouldn't catch him staring like some creep.

"I should still let you get to your meal." Carly turned her horse with the slightest motion of the reins. Nieve instantly moved on cue, turning back toward their property. "It was nice meeting you both."

"You too, Miss Hawkins," Oscar called out as she started to trot away.

"Call me Carly," she told Oscar over her shoulder. She glanced once more at Jesse and said, "See you around?"

"See you around," he confirmed.

It sounded like a promise. One he was very tempted to keep.

Chapter Three

As Jesse and Oscar headed back to Grayson's, Jesse's mind was stuck on rewind, replaying that meeting with Carly again and again. For the first time in a very long time, he felt something that he thought abandoned him long ago.

Interest.

It had felt like forever since a woman had made him feel even remotely that *spark*. In the span of a few minutes, Jesse had gone through rampant emotions: surprise, amusement, horror, and…desire. It wasn't just that she was a beautiful woman with a smile that could stop a wild mustang in its tracks. It was the way she'd reacted when Oscar practically shouted statistics at her. A lot of people were easily put off by his son's ramblings, especially when he went off on one of his streaks.

It was one of the main reasons Jesse had decided to move them to Tenacity. While Oscar's school in Houston might have had better resources to help him with his autism, he had started to become distant, not only with his fellow students but with Jesse. It wasn't easy for his son to make friends, and he'd practically disappeared in the large high school's population. The only people who seemed to notice him were the bullies who made fun of the sensory headphones that he sometimes wore to stop himself from getting overstimulated.

After an especially tough day at school where someone had hidden Oscar's headphones and he'd had a meltdown in the middle of class, Jesse had called his brother, Grayson. As soon as he'd heard his brother's voice, Jesse had spewed out all his concerns. It was most of the usual: He was failing as a father, neither of them were doing well, MaryBeth was the only one who could reach their son.

Grayson had let out a soft sigh when he was done before saying, *Jess... I think a visit to Tenacity would be good for you and Oscar.*

After Jesse had hung up the phone, he'd taken a long, hard look around his house. Not much had changed since MaryBeth had died. Her favorite pictures of them decorated the walls, and the blanket she would curl up under during the winter evenings still had its space on the back of the couch. If he walked into the kitchen, he knew he'd find all of her favorite recipe books on the shelf above the refrigerator, collecting dust. He'd never gotten rid of them, though Lord knew when was the last time anyone touched them. He made simple food for himself and his son: hamburgers, spaghetti with sauce out of a jar, and Friday night's splurge featuring either pizza or fast food. He'd be the first to admit that the family of two had been living in a rut since their center died.

And he'd thought...maybe for both of their sakes, something needed to change. A few months later, he'd enrolled Oscar into Tenacity High School, and they officially moved to town.

He figured the smaller, quieter setting would be good for Oscar. Maybe his son would have a chance to make a friend or two. But Jesse knew it was also time for himself to start moving on. It had been nearly ten years since MaryBeth had died, and while he'd had the occasional one-night stand, it wasn't his style to casually date. Just because he was half tempted to turn his horse around so he could hopefully run into Carly again didn't mean anything. He needed to make sure Oscar was succeeding in his new environment first before he even considered dating someone. When he was finally ready to get back in the market, he wouldn't date a woman whose whole career was living on the edge and risking her life. He didn't want to fall for someone he could easily lose with one stumble of a horse. So, there was no point in thinking about a certain internationally famous rodeo star any further.

It was as they were entering the padlock on Grayson's property that he realized Oscar was quiet—too quiet for someone who'd just met a professional athlete and rattled off her stats. When he glanced over at his son, he caught Oscar staring at him.

"What?" he finally asked.

Oscar gave him a pointed look. "You missed the turn to the barn."

"What? No I—" Jesse looked toward Grayson's property and saw that his horse had led him down another trail instead of toward the homestead. He halted the animal and glanced over to where Oscar was stopped at the fork in the paths, waiting for his father to rejoin him.

"You're distracted," Oscar concluded.

"No, I'm not," Jesse muttered as he turned his horse around so they could get back on the right track.

Right before they reached the barn, they came to another stop.

Jesse had just swung his leg over the horse when Oscar said, "You should ask Carly Hawkins out."

Jesse was so startled that his foot caught in the stirrup and he almost fell onto his butt. He thankfully caught himself before hitting the ground. Meanwhile, his son gracefully hopped off his own horse, patting the mare on the side of her face before leading her into the barn.

Collecting himself, Jesse followed suit. "What are you talking about?"

"Pleeeeease, Dad. You were practically drooling."

"I was not!" Jesse grumbled, leading his mare to the cross-tie area so he could take off the tack.

They worked in silence for several minutes as they each took care of their horses.

They carried the saddles into the tack room, the sharp scent of leather and saddle soap filling the air. Dust motes drifted lazily through the shafts of afternoon sunlight cutting across the space. The day's ride had left both of them sweaty and tired, but the familiar routine of cleaning the tack relaxed Jesse.

Oscar broke the silence first. "It's okay, you know."

He glanced at his son. "What's okay?"

"If you want to ask Carly out." Oscar said it so casually, like he was commenting on the weather. "She's single, you know. She was dating Fletch Alistair, but they broke up. Probably 'cause he's not a very good bull rider."

Jesse's hand stilled mid-motion, the rag half-draped over his saddle horn. He tried to play it off, focusing on a stubborn bit of dirt on the stirrup leather. "That so?"

Oscar shrugged. "Yeah. I saw it on Australian YouTube. It was all over the news over there."

"Why are you watching Australian YouTu— You know

what? Never mind." Jesse's pulse kicked up a notch at the confirmation—Carly was single—but he tamped it down just as fast. He wasn't some lovesick teenager. "I'm not interested in dating Carly, or anyone else, so it doesn't matter," he said, a little too quickly.

Oscar didn't seem convinced. His brow furrowed as he went to the utility sink, the faucet squealing in protest as he turned it on. He soaked a cloth and wrung it out, then came back to his saddle. "You don't think she's hot? I mean—for an old person?"

Jesse huffed, a laugh escaping before he could stop it. "Old person, huh? She's what, thirty?"

"Exactly," Oscar said, as if that proved his point. "Basically ancient."

"Careful," Jesse warned lightly, running a hand along the saddle's flank. "By your standards, I'm prehistoric."

Oscar grinned. "You said it, not me."

Jesse shook his head, hiding a smile. He focused on the saddle again, but Carly's name lingered in his mind longer than he wanted to admit. *No*, he told himself firmly. He didn't have time for that kind of complication.

But as the silence stretched between them again, the thud of cloth on leather rhythmic and steady, the thought stayed anyway. "Yes, she's very pretty." *Pretty* didn't even describe how beautiful the woman was, but hadn't Jesse just told himself that he wasn't going to think about her anymore?

Oscar. Focus on Oscar.

"Enough about my love life," Jesse said.

"What love life?" Oscar muttered. "You need to get a life so you don't worry so much about mine."

He ignored that. "And on that note, what's going on with you? Is school getting any better?"

His son's face soured for a second before it brightened again. "Coach Finn is great."

Jesse would always be grateful that Finn Monahan had bonded with Oscar over football and had encouraged the teen to be part of the football team in his own way. The kid was like a sponge—absorbing anything sports related that he could. Football was something he could talk about to anyone who'd listen. Finn was a former NFL quarterback and respected Oscar's knowledge. But would the students his age give him a chance to talk?

As they left the barn and started heading toward the house, they could hear the children of Grayson's girlfriend, JenniLynn Garrett, yelling from inside.

Jesse winced at the noise before checking to make sure Oscar wasn't getting overly stimulated. Oscar's hands clenched and unclenched, a sign that he was starting to stim.

"Where are your headphones?" Jesse asked.

"In my bedroom," Oscar said. "It's fine—"

"Stay here. I'll go get them," he insisted.

As he hurried into the house, he remembered why he didn't date anyone seriously. Oscar was his main focus. Jesse was all Oscar had. And he needed to remember that.

Two days later, Jesse was hammering a fence post in place. His back ached and his shirt was soaked with sweat, but he only had a few more to install and then he could get the barbed wiring done. It felt strange to get back to ranching after living in the city for so long. He'd worked in an office, doing analytical work. He'd hated it, but it kept him in Houston, which was where Mary-Beth had grown up.

The truth was he'd missed this life. There was nothing better than being out in the fresh air at the crack of dawn, making sure the animals were fed and cared for. After he and Oscar had made the decision to move to Tenacity, Jesse had been more than a little excited to leave the corporate world behind and all the stress that came with it.

He wanted to get back to his roots. While he still did remote IT work, he was counting the minutes until he could finish the house, quit his job, and get back to full-time ranching. Some of his fondest memories included following his dad around their property when he was a kid and helping with chores. Jesse hoped Oscar would love it as much as he had.

The conversation he and Oscar had the other day popped into his head. He couldn't believe his son actually encouraged him to ask Carly Hawkins out. He didn't plan on doing it. He had to focus on his ranch and making sure he hadn't made the biggest mistake of his life dragging Oscar out to the country. He wanted his son to be happy and to have the world at his feet. But the world didn't exactly come crawling to Tenacity, Montana.

Though…that hadn't stopped a beautiful, worldly woman like Carly from moving to town.

As much as he wanted to pretend otherwise, he couldn't stop thinking of her. Just hearing her voice for those precious few minutes made him want to smile. A woman like her could have her choice of men. He seriously doubted that she'd want to give a single dad like him a shot. Hell, he didn't even have his own roof over his head yet.

Jesse scowled as he took off his cowboy hat and wiped

at his sweaty forehead with the back of his arm. Even though fall was right around the corner, it was still warm. He put the Stetson back on and was about to reach for the final post when he heard a vehicle coming down the dirt road that split his property from Grayson's. A familiar truck came to a halt in front of him, and his brother rolled down his window.

"Hey, man," Grayson said as he came to a halt. He looked down the line of fencing that Jesse had been working on. "Things are looking good."

Jesse glanced at his project, his mind still occupied with Carly. "Thanks. The contractors are working on the electrical at the house and seeing as that's not my specialty, I figured I'd work on some exterior projects."

Grayson was silent for a moment before he said, "What's wrong with you?"

"Nothing," he muttered as he grabbed his mallet off the ground so he could whack the post a few more times.

"You sure? 'Cause you look like a thunderstorm is headed our way."

"It's nothing. Just something Oscar said the other day."

Grayson put his truck in Park before turning his full attention back to his brother. "Hit me."

Jesse ran his fingers over the smooth top of the mallet. "Do you know Carly Hawkins?"

Grayson's eyebrows pulled together. "Not well, though I heard she bought the property next to mine, so I'm sure it's only a matter of time before JenniLynn invites her over." He sounded grumpy, though the fondness in his eyes when mentioning his girlfriend revealed he wasn't really upset. He usually wasn't when it came to her.

"We ran into Carly when we took the horses out the

other day…" Jesse went on to explain the encounter with the woman he couldn't forget.

Grayson smirked when he was finished. "Oscar get a little crush on her?"

Jesse set the mallet on the post. "No. He said I should ask her out."

"Oh…" Grayson said, his expression not holding back his surprise. Jesse didn't blame him.

"I know. It's a ridiculous idea." He went over to the pile of posts he'd set out earlier and bent down to grab one.

"Why is it ridiculous?" Grayson asked.

Jesse straightened to look at his brother. "You know why." He lifted his work-gloved hand and starting counting off. "For one, she's a famous rodeo star. Two, did you forget about Oscar? I can't date right now. He just started at a new school."

"Finn told me he's keeping Oscar under his wing," Grayson said.

A lump formed in Jesse's throat. He hadn't realized his brother was talking to the school's football coach and looking out for his nephew.

"All things considered Oscar's a pretty independent kid. He might need a little wiggle room to get his feet under him in school."

Jesse opened his mouth to argue that but instead said, "That doesn't change the fact that Carly is a huge star."

"You can still ask the woman out," Grayson responded. "What's the worst she can say? No, right? At least you'll know."

Yeah. That actually sounded horrible. Jesse glared at the remaining posts.

"Is this about MaryBeth?" Grayson asked, his tone careful.

Jesse's throat bobbed, but he didn't answer.

His brother let out a sad sigh. "She wouldn't want you to grow old alone."

"I know," Jesse replied after swallowing hard. He stared at the ground. "She was always so good with Oscar. Do you remember how she could calm him with just a look? I feel like I screw up all the time with him."

"You're not. He's a good kid who handles situations a little differently—that's all. You deserve to be happy. You both do." Grayson reached for the gearshift and put it back into Drive. "Ask the woman out, Jess. And if she says no, JenniLynn is the mayor. She knows literally everyone in this town. She can find you a nice woman to date."

He waved at Jesse before continuing down the road.

Jesse's mind raced with everything that his brother said, but one thing stood out—that Grayson offered to set Jesse up with someone. He'd need to put an end to that. It was bad enough whenever he made a trip to town for something that the single women circled him like sharks. He didn't need his family setting him up with some random woman. He certainly didn't want it to get around town that he was open to dating.

Because if Jesse was going to ask out anyone, it would be the one he couldn't stop thinking about. The one who made his pulse jump just by thinking of her. The one he shouldn't have. She was off-limits, and he needed to remember to keep it that way.

So why was it that every time he told himself to forget her, she found a way to slip back into his thoughts?

Chapter Four

Carly chewed on her lip as she waited for her cousin Remi to answer her front door. Remi's fiancé, Shane Corey, was the one who opened it, looking like he was on his way out.

"Hey, Carly," he said. "You here to distract Remi, I hope?"

Carly laughed. "Maybe. Does she need a distraction?"

"Tiffany sent over *another* floral design for her to consider for the wedding," he said, mentioning Tiffany Brandt, who was engaged to his brother, Ellis. The brothers and their fiancées had decided to have a dual wedding. Carly didn't know how they were going to pull it off, but she wished them luck. Shane continued, "This is the eighth one this week. I think Remi's getting a little overwhelmed. I asked her if she wanted scrambled or fried eggs this morning, and I thought she was going to have a conniption."

Carly did her best to keep her face straight. "I'll see what I can do to help."

"Awesome," Shane said. "I need to go check on the border fence. I'll see you later."

She waved goodbye to him before entering the house. She could hear Remi muttering to herself somewhere within, and she followed the noise until she came upon her cousin pacing back and forth in her family room.

"Hi," Carly greeted.

Remi turned to face her. Her eyes were red rimmed like she hadn't slept in a week, and her hair was sticking up at the crown of her head. "Did you know there are over a hundred shades of pink roses? How am I supposed to pick the correct shade?"

Carly walked over to her cousin and grabbed her hands. "Honey, I need you to breathe with me." She inhaled deeply, and Remi copied the motion before they exhaled in unison. "Whatever shade you pick will be perfect. Honestly, it won't matter in the end because the only thing that Shane cares about is marrying you. You could show up in jean shorts carrying a bouquet of dandelions for all that matters to him."

Remi took another deep breath to steady herself. "Yeah. You're right. I just want everything to be perfect."

"It will be."

"Thanks, cuz." Remi beamed at her before tilting her head. "Not that I don't appreciate you talking me down from the proverbial ledge, but what are you doing here?"

"Um..." Carly fiddled with the end of her ponytail. "I was wondering if you knew a place I could buy baked goods. And then I wanted to ask if you knew the best way to get to Jesse Abernathy's place over on Ambling Hills."

Remi's jaw dropped. "Okay...why do you need to know those things?"

"I was out riding Nieve the other day, and I accidentally went onto the Abernathy property and ran into Jesse and his son. I thought they were on my property though, and I was a little passive-aggressive, if you want to call it that."

Remi snorted. "Knowing you, I'd say that's a fair term."

Carly gave her a mock glare. "Anyway, he was really nice about the misunderstanding, but I feel like I should still be neighborly and offer him a peace offering."

Remi tapped her chin thoughtfully before blurting excitedly, "Oh my God, do you have a crush on him? Does Amy know?"

Carly's cheeks burned. "I do not have a crush. Thirty-year-olds do not have crushes."

"Sure they do. Is he good looking?"

"I…" Carly was going to deny it, but given the knowing look Remi was sending her, she caved. "Yes, he's sinfully good looking, with eyes like sea glass and light brown hair. He's absolutely gorgeous."

"Okay, then. Here's what we're going to do," Remi said. "We're going to go into town, and we'll see if Betty's Bakehouse has any whole pies to sell. If not, the grocery store will probably have cookies or something available. Let's go."

"Uh… Remi?" Carly said.

"Hmm?" Remi replied. She seemed to be looking for something. She started mumbling, "Where'd I put that purse?"

"Do you maybe want to brush your hair and put on some fresh clothes first?" Carly said as delicately as possible.

Remi frowned as she looked down at herself. She had baby's breath sticking to her yoga pants from one of the flower bundles lying on the floor and a stain from who knew what on her shirt.

"Give me twenty minutes to take a shower and put on fresh clothes."

"You've got it," Carly replied, full of love for her family. How had she gone so long without them?

An hour later, they were pulling into Betty's Bakehouse.

"Have you tried the desserts here yet?" Remi asked as they got out of the car.

"Nope," Carly replied as they entered the cute bakery. A long glass counter filled with doughnuts and baked goods ran along the wall opposite of the main door. The whole place smelled like dough and sugar, causing Carly's mouth to water.

"I'll be right with you," a woman called out from the back.

"Take your time," Remi replied.

The baker finally came to the front, a splotch of flour on her cheek. "Remi! What brings you in today?"

"Hi, Betty," she said. "This is my cousin Carly, and she needs to buy a pie. One that says *Sorry I was a douche to you.*"

"Remi!" Carly said, burying her face in her hands.

"Male or female?" Betty asked matter-of-factly.

"Male," Remi answered. "And hot as sin too."

"Remember that nice moment we had earlier?" Carly grumbled. "I'm taking it back."

"You love me and you know it," Remi replied.

Betty looked thoughtful before she turned and waved to a glass display cabinet. It was loaded with mouthwatering desserts.

"We don't serve humble pie," Betty said, causing Remi to snort. "But we do offer a delicious apple."

"We'll take it," Carly said, wanting nothing more than to get out of the situation.

Betty grabbed one from the case and put it on the counter for Carly to approve. It looked amazing, and she quickly paid for it so that they could leave.

"Who's the lucky man?" the baker asked as she handed Carly the pie.

"Oh, it's nothing," Carly insisted as she took it from the waitress. "Just my apology for being a douche, like Remi said."

Remi looked like she was about to burst from holding in her laughter.

"Anyway, we should go," Carly said, her ears burning.

"Come see us again soon," Betty replied, looking more than a little amused. They waved goodbye and hurried outside.

"I cannot believe you said all that," Carly said under her breath when she and Remi made their way back to the car.

"It was going to be all over town anyway that you were buying a mystery gift for someone. Might as well rip the Band-Aid off now and give the gossips some fat to chew on."

Carly rolled her eyes, but a part of her worried if that was true. What if the press got a hold of it? *Carly Hawkins breaks Fletch Alistair's heart for hot Montana cowboy.*

Her agent, Dex, would have a panic attack.

She didn't want to deal with the press again anytime soon. Despite her best efforts, she thought back to that time after she and Fletch broke up. The media had gotten so ugly. The paparazzi had been relentless, following her everywhere. She couldn't deny that they were a tiny part of why she'd decided to leave Australia. She'd be perfectly fine if she never had a camera shoved in her face again.

When Remi started driving toward Ambling Hills instead of back to her house for Carly to get her car, Carly snapped back to attention. "Wait, where are you going?"

"You didn't think I was going to miss this, did you?" Remi said. "Besides, you said you wanted to distract me. Color me entertained."

Carly leaned back in the passenger seat and closed her eyes, accepting defeat. "Let's just get this done."

They eventually turned down the only road that ran along Ambling Hills. On one side of the road was a fenced-in area that had cattle roaming freely. On the other side was a half-assembled fence.

"This is all Grayson Abernathy's property," Remi explained. "It was really nice of him to let his brother have a piece of land."

"Yeah, it was." It warmed Carly that Jesse came from a family like that, and then she scolded herself. She was only here to apologize and then move on with her life.

The land grew more structured as they came up to a small house on the hill. In the distance, she could see two men hammering vinyl siding on one part of the house. They were both about the same height with the same color hair.

"Looks like Grayson is here too," Remi said as she pulled up the driveway.

"Awesome," Carly mumbled. One more person there to witness her eat crow.

Once they were parked, Remi winked at her. "Go get 'em."

"What? After all this, you're not coming with me?"

"I'm just here for moral support," Remi replied, her face angelic. "You've got this."

Carly glowered at her. "Thanks." But she couldn't help the snort that slipped out when Remi winked back.

She got out of the car, careful not to dump the pie. As she headed toward the house, one of the men came toward her. He looked like Jesse. It had to be his brother.

"Hello," she said.

"Can I help you?" His face was polite, even as his eyes drifted down to what she was holding. He did a double take, as though it was unusual for a strange woman to show up at a construction site bearing pie. Which was completely fair.

Carly bit her lip at how ridiculous she was starting to feel. "Uh… I was hoping I could speak to Jesse?" she said.

The man she figured was Grayson nodded before calling out, "Jess, there's someone with pie here to see you."

She resisted the urge to bury her face in said pie, but she stopped thinking completely when Jesse came around the corner. He didn't see her at first because he was using the end of his T-shirt to wipe the sweat off his brow, putting his abs on full display.

"What?" he said, his voice muffled.

"Stop showing off the six-pack," the lookalike told him.

Six-pack? Try a twenty-four-pack. Lordy.

Jesse finally pulled his shirt away and glanced at Carly. He immediately dropped his shirt, to her disappointment. "Carly?" he said.

"Hi," she replied.

"Hi." He took a couple of hesitant steps toward her. "Grayson, this is Carly Hawkins. Our new neighbor."

"Howdy," Grayson said, and she smiled politely at him. He turned to Jesse. "I'm going to start measuring out the rest of that board."

He disappeared around the corner, leaving Jesse and Carly momentarily alone. She wished she'd dressed a little nicer. She had on an old T-shirt with the Australian Rodeo Circuit logo on it, capris, and flip-flops. Her hair was in its usual ponytail. She had been determined when she'd left the house to make her apologies and leave, so she had no reason to dress to impress. And even though he was wearing a T-shirt that had seen better days, she felt like a toad next to him. Not that she wanted to make a better impression or anything. Nope, this was simply a visit to be a good neighbor and make sure she didn't set off on the wrong foot with the Abernathys. From what Amy had told her, his family had a lot of influence in Montana.

She glanced at the house. "This is nice. It's going to be really cute when it's done."

"Thanks," Jesse finally said. "So…what brings you out this way?"

"Hmm? Oh!" Carly hurried up to him and handed him the pie. "I wanted to give you this."

Jesse looked down at it. "An apple pie?"

"More of what I'd call an apology pie."

Jesse glanced back at her, his eyes crinkling in the corners. Damn, he was good looking. "No need to apologize again. You didn't know you had crossed onto our property."

"I don't just mean for not knowing directions very

well. I felt like I was a little rude to you, and I wanted to apologize for that."

Jesse's eyes seemed to see right inside of her. He gave her an understanding look. "I get it. Women these days have to be extra cautious, especially in the woods. If I'd known we were about to cross paths, I would have made my presence known long before I did."

"Regardless, I could have been nicer."

He flashed a dimpled smile at her. "We'll have to agree to disagree on that."

She grinned back. "Deal."

"Still…" he said, looking back at the gift. "You didn't need to bake me a pie."

She laughed. She couldn't help herself. "That's courtesy of Betty's Bakery. Trust me, you don't want me anywhere near a kitchen. Last time I tried to cook anything, I gave myself food poisoning."

Jesse's smile widened. "Noted."

"Well…" Carly said. "I should let you get back to what you were doing."

He lifted the pie. "Thanks again for dessert."

"You're welcome." She nodded awkwardly and then hurried back to Remi's car, even though she really didn't want to leave him just yet. It was the silliest thing. This was only the second time she'd met the man. There was no reason to feel like her feet were filling with lead with each step she took away from him.

As she settled in the car, she realized that he was still watching her. She waved at him before buckling her seat belt. She forced her eyes straight ahead, not daring to look his way again.

Remi started the vehicle, and they drove in silence for several seconds.

Her cousin finally said, “Damn, Carly.”

“I know,” Carly muttered.

“Sinfully hot.”

“Yep,” she replied.

“What are you going to do about that?”

What was she going to do? Absolutely nothing. Hadn't she been telling herself since she moved to Tenacity that she needed to figure out the next steps in her life? It hadn't even been a year since her breakup with Fletch made national news. She didn't need to rush into anything new. Carly wanted to focus on herself.

Not on the man's dimples or the way his hair curled at the ends or…

Carly slouched in her seat and closed her eyes.

She was so totally screwed.

Chapter Five

Carly casually glanced around the high school football stadium. It was packed, but that had a lot to do with the home team being on a winning streak. When she'd called Amy the day before to ask what her plans were for that Friday night, Amy had joked that she was going to live it up as one did in a small town and go watch the local football team. When she mentioned that Remi and Shane were also going, Carly decided to join the family festivities. Though she may have had alternative reasons for wanting to be there.

"Who are you looking for?" Amy asked.

Carly tried not to look like a kid stealing from the cookie jar as she quickly said, "No one!"

Remi turned where she sat on the bleacher in the row below. She eyed her knowingly. "You're looking for Mr. Hot and Sweaty."

"Who?" Amy asked. Her gaze narrowed on Carly. "You didn't tell me there was a guy."

"That's because there *isn't* one," Carly insisted.

"Oh, there's a guy," Remi said. "And the way they looked at each other…" Remi fanned herself. "I'd say love is in the air."

Carly gave her cousin a dry look. "You got all that from an apology pie?"

"I'm so lost right now," Amy complained before looking at their cousin. "Since she's being tightlipped about it, I'll need you to fill me in."

"Ugh," Carly muttered. She palmed her face, hiding her eyes as Remi gave Amy an exaggerated account of what happened.

"And then Carly practically jumped him," Remi continued.

"I did not!" she said.

"You wanted to."

Thankfully, her cousin caught sight of her fiancé, and her voice trailed off as she took in her own man. Shane carried a tray full of snacks from the concession stand. Amy's husband, Josh, followed behind, carrying a container of drinks. Remi catcalled Shane, whose face lit up at the sight of her. He and Josh made their way up the stands toward them.

Amy lightly elbowed Carly. "Tell me your version."

Carly lifted a shoulder. "There really isn't much to tell. I ran into this guy and his son the other day on the trails. We spoke for a second, and then I realized I was trespassing, so I got out of Dodge. I was a little rude during our encounter, so I took him an apple pie to apologize. That's all that happened."

"And you think he's attractive."

"She may have mentioned ocean-colored eyes," Remi said. "I believe that was a direct quote."

"Hey!" Carly lightly tapped her cousin's backside with her foot.

"Are we talking about the guy Carly thinks is hot?"

Shane said as he sat next to Remi, brushing his lips against her temples.

"Oh for Pete's sake." Carly looked up to the sky. "You make me sound like a schoolgirl with a crush."

"We're just giving you a hard time. It's really sweet," Remi said, taking the food off the tray Shane had, then passing a bucket of popcorn to Amy. "We're really excited to see you having a life outside of the rodeo. Maybe this is an opportunity to put down some roots?"

"What! There are no roots to put down with this guy. I—" Carly's mouth dropped as the man in question approached where she was sitting. He was walking behind a woman with three girls, a boy, and Grayson.

"Hello, Mayor!" Josh called out.

The woman looked up, waving to them. "Hello! It's good to see you all. Thanks for coming out to support our boys."

"They're going to go all the way this year!" Shane said before grumbling under his breath, "They better. I've got twenty dollars on it."

Remi gave her fiancé a mock glare. "That money could have gone toward the wedding."

Shane wiggled his brows at her. "Don't worry. I took it out of the bachelor party fund."

Carly only half listened to their exchange, her focus locked on Jesse. He was dressed casually in a light gray sweatshirt that shaped him and worn jeans that looked soft to the touch. He was just as handsome as she remembered. More so under the lights of the stadium. He hadn't noticed her yet. He was staring at the team on the field where they were warming up, a frown on his handsome face.

Amy noticed her staring and cranked her head to look at Jesse. "Is that him? Please tell me that's him. He's delicious."

"Um, hi, remember me?" Josh teased.

"Of course, and *obviously* he's not as handsome as you," Amy assured, kissing her husband on the cheek. She turned back to Carly. "But is that him?"

Carly's face heated. Her family didn't know the meaning of the word *subtle*. "Yes, and please lower your voice. The stadium announcer isn't as loud as you."

"That's Grayson Abernathy's brother," Shane remarked, joining the conversation. "He and his kid recently moved to town, but he's a bit of a loner."

"Is he married?" Remi asked.

"Don't know," Shane replied. "All I heard was that he moved in with his brother and he's building himself a house on the other side of the Abernathy ranch."

Carly's heart thumped at that. What was Jesse's story? There hadn't been a wife riding with them the other day, but that didn't mean there wasn't one. Maybe she hadn't moved to town yet because she was closing up their house back from wherever they used to live.

Embarrassment made Carly wince. What his wife must have thought of her if she found out Carly had brought her husband a pie. Carly had been so focused on not being a bad neighbor that she hadn't given a thought to the fact that he might be married.

She closed her eyes. That'd be all she needed—for the news to pick up that storyline... *After ugly breakup with Fletch Alistair, Carly Hawkins sets eyes on married man.*

"Are you worried about Oscar's mom?" Remi asked as if reading her thoughts.

"No… I mean, it doesn't matter. It's not like I'm about to date the man or something."

Amy cocked her head, her eyes squinting. "I don't see a wedding ring."

Carly quirked an eyebrow. "How many ranchers do you know who wear wedding rings? It's a bit of a hazard, isn't it? Last thing they need is for the ring to get caught on equipment or they get ring avulsion because some steer ripped it off their finger."

"If you're worried about it, just ask the man," Amy replied.

"What if they had a horrible breakup?" Carly said. "That'll be a great way to sour any potential romance. Or worse. What if she died or something? I don't want to bring up any bad memories."

"Maybe he's a criminal on the run," Remi joked. "And he has a woman in every city. Oscar's mom could be one of many women he left behind."

Carly gave her a sardonic look. "Thanks for that."

"You need to stop reading those dark romances you've gotten into lately," Amy told their cousin as she reached for a handful of popcorn.

Carly's face scrunched. "When did you start reading dark romance?"

"I needed something to distract myself from all the wedding chaos. Faith suggested a particular book, and I've been down a rabbit hole ever since," Remi explained, mentioning Amy and Carly's sister. She gave Amy a sly smile. "I'm happy to loan you a few books if you need something to spice up your life. Trust me, Shane *loves* some of the ideas I discovered in these stories."

"My life is spicy enough, thank you very much," Amy replied.

"Amen to that," Josh said. He picked up her hand and kissed the back of it, making Amy blush.

Thankfully the whistle blew announcing the start of the game.

"Later," she mumbled. But she knew she wouldn't. Because as much as she found Jesse Abernathy attractive, there was no way that man was single.

The crowd around Jesse went wild as Tenacity High's football team scored another touchdown. He didn't notice the score. He was too busy watching Oscar. His son stood off to the side of the rest of the team, holding water bottles ready to hand out if anyone asked. No one did. Either the boys on the team were too engrossed in the game or they were too busy flirting with the cheerleaders. Coach Finn finally called out to Oscar, and his son hurried over to the man.

"You breathing over there?" Grayson joked.

Jesse turned to see Grayson and JenniLynn staring at him. JenniLynn's youngest daughter, Hallie, bounced on her lap while her other daughters, Lila and Sasha, played on the bench next to her. Grayson's son, Adam, was the only one watching the game.

"Yeah, everything's fine," Jesse answered.

"Finn's keeping an eye on him," JenniLynn assured him.

Sure enough, the coach said something close to Oscar's ear before patting him on the back. Jesse wasn't sure what the exchange was about, but Oscar perked up, his shoulders straightening before he pointed toward the field. His son looked happy in that moment, and the strain in Jesse's shoulders loosened.

He glanced at the scoreboard and realized it was almost halftime. He could understand the excitement in the air. The home team was crushing it.

Jesse leaned back on his palms and glanced around. He straightened when he noticed Carly Hawkins in the section over. He'd been so focused on making sure Oscar was okay that he hadn't even realized the woman who'd been taking up most of his brain cells since he met her was right near him.

As if feeling his eyes on her, Carly glanced over. Her eyes widened when she realized he was staring. His hand seemed to raise of its own accord and started to wave at her like a lunatic before he forced it back down. She smiled before turning to listen to the woman who was speaking adamantly beside her.

"Uncle Jesse, you're being super cringe," JenniLynn's oldest daughter, Lila, said.

Jesse winced. "Yeah, I know."

He forced himself to watch the marching band, who was now on the field since it was officially halftime. The instruments were bright and shiny under the stadium lights, distracting the attendees from how awful they sounded. Oscar had gone off to the locker room with the rest of the team. Jesse couldn't resist looking at Carly again. The woman in front of her was turned almost fully around, talking fast. Carly shook her head, her lips pursing.

"Isn't that the woman who gave you a pie the other day?" Grayson asked.

"Yeah," Jesse muttered.

"Oh! That's the Hawkins sister. She just moved here," JenniLynn said. "I think her name is Caroline. No, Cassidy. No—"

"Carly," Jesse corrected.

"That's right." JenniLynn leaned over to get a better look at the group across the way. "She's beautiful. Are you planning on giving her heart-eyes from a distance all night, or are you going to do something about it?"

"What?" Jesse jerked his gaze back to his family. "I don't know what you're talking about."

JenniLynn gave him a no-nonsense look.

"We're saying go ask the woman out," Grayson said. He gave Jesse a shove. "Go on."

"What? Now?" Jesse said, low-key panicking. He'd been planning what he'd say to Carly if he ever ran into her again. Something smooth that would immediately have her falling head over heels for him. Because while his brain couldn't let go of what she did for a living, his heart was reminding him of something else—that he still had one. He knew that for a fact because every time he thought of the woman lately, the organ beat harder in his chest. It was unfortunate that he couldn't think of a single pickup line he'd had memorized.

"Go on," JenniLynn encouraged, "before someone else gets to her first."

Jesse's gaze shot back to Carly. Sure enough, there were about four cowboys surrounding her, eyeing her up.

Oh hell no.

Jesse jumped to his feet and made his way through the crowd. Before he knew it, he was standing in front of the woman.

Carly wasn't wearing her cowgirl hat tonight. Her long

brown hair was piled into a bun on top of her head with loose strands framing her face. Under the stadium lighting, he could pick out coppery undertones. He was half tempted to reach out and trace them with his fingers.

"Hi, Jesse," Carly said when he continued to stand there like a man whose brain left the building.

"Hi," he practically shouted, inwardly wincing when her family turned to stare at him with varying looks of disbelief, amusement, and judgment—the latter especially on the faces of the women. "I, um, I noticed you and thought I should do the neighborly thing and say hello."

She smiled, and he was struck dumb again. "I appreciate that. How was the pie?"

"It was great. Thank you again for it."

She nodded, and he scrambled to think of something else to say. The whistle blew, indicating the game was back on. And thank God for that.

"Well…" he said. Without another word he turned around and scurried back to his section of the bleachers.

JenniLynn and Grayson both looked like they were about to burst out laughing.

"So…" Grayson finally said. "How'd it go?"

"Shut up," Jesse grumbled. He almost wished a tornado would appear so he could have a reason to scurry away.

When the game finally came to a merciful end, he trailed after his family as they made their way out of the stadium. He'd told Oscar that they'd wait for him at the entrance. Because it was just that kind of night, he and Carly met at the end of the bleachers. He'd done his best not to look at her for the rest of the game, but it'd been almost painful to resist. The few times he'd risked looking at her, he could see the females in her family laughing and giving her a hard time about something. He almost hoped, and dreaded, that their conversation was about him.

Her expression warmed upon seeing him, and despite how things had gone earlier, he was in front of her before he knew it.

"Listen," he said. "Sorry about earlier. I'm not usually so—"

"Lost for words?" She smirked. "Don't worry about it."

"Yeah, I mean…" *To hell with it.* "Would you like to go out with me sometime? I clearly need practice communicating with people. Other than my teenage son."

"And you want me to teach you?" She laughed. The sound was like music to his ears. "Well, that's a pickup line that I haven't heard before. Well played."

The corner of his mouth tilted up. It wasn't the one of the many pickup lines he'd practiced all week, but he wasn't about to look a gift horse in the mouth. "Soooo… is that a yes?"

"Yes, that sounds nice," she replied. "Here, hand me your phone."

As he watched her add her name to his list of contacts, a movement caught his eye. He looked over and saw one of the football players hand his water jug to Oscar, who dropped it, spilling water all over his shoes. The football player joined his friends, not noticing their waterboy or the mess. Oscar stared at his feet and started to clench and unclench his hands—a sign he was starting to stim.

"Here you go," Carly said, handing the phone back to him. "I'm looking forward to—"

"Great. I'll call you," Jesse said. He hurried for the exit so he could get to his son before Oscar had a meltdown. He missed the hurt expression on Carly's face as he left.

Chapter Six

Jesse stood in his Houston home four days later, staring at Carly's phone number. He'd pulled up the number at least a dozen times since she'd given it to him. He'd even thought of messaging her, just to say hey, but everything he'd come up with to send her sounded dumb. He hadn't dated anyone in so long. He wasn't sure what was acceptable or not.

Did he tell her that he couldn't stop thinking about her? Doubtful. He'd come across as a stalker.

He thought about *Hey, it's Jesse. Let me give you a night on the town.* But Tenacity wasn't that big of a town, and did it come across as too cocky? He didn't want to blow this.

"God, you are bad at this," he muttered.

Sighing, he did the one thing he really knew he shouldn't. He pulled up the group chat he had with his siblings and started typing.

How soon should you follow up with someone these days after you ask them on a date?

He stared at it, debating if he should send it or not, before finally saying, "To hell with it," and then hit Send.

He watched as multiple dots started appearing indicating several people were typing.

Jonathan: You dating again, bro? Congrats!

Amanda: I'm so happy for you, Jess!

Benjamin: Is she hot?

Amanda: It doesn't matter if she's hot or not. Is she a good person?

Benjamin: *eye-roll emoji*

Grayson: You STILL haven't followed up with Carly?

Amanda: Have you met her, Gray? What's she like?

Jonathan: How long's it been?

Grayson: Four days! And yes, she's cool. She brought Jesse a pie.

Benjamin: Dude! Four days?

Jesse: Thanks for that, Gray.

Grayson: Hey, little bro, you came to us.

Jesse: Reminder that I'm the second oldest here.

Jonathan: Then act it, man.

Amanda: I don't get the pie reference, but if you're interested, call the woman now.

Benjamin: Hopefully she still remembers you.

Amanda: Stop scaring him. Jess, it's great you're starting to date again. It's time.

Jonathan: Yeah, we're happy for you, bro.

Benjamin: But four days???

Amanda: Okay, so that's not ideal.

Jesse felt a little queasy. Had he messed this up already? He was in the process of asking that when their youngest sister finally entered the chat.

Evie: Man up or shut up. Some of us are trying to sleep!!!

Jesse scowled as he shoved his phone back into his pocket. His family was right. Jesse felt like a heel because he'd asked Carly out and then hadn't found the time to speak with her. He'd had to drive down to his former home and empty the rest of it out.

He'd put off the task for as long as he could. He hadn't wanted to leave Oscar, but he also hadn't wanted to take him out of school. He knew it was best for Oscar to keep him in his routine. But he hadn't left his son this long in his entire life. It had taken Grayson and JenniLynn a full two days to convince him that they'd guard him with their lives while Jesse was gone, to reassure him that he could make this trip. He also found that now that they'd sold the house and the new owners took over the next week, he wasn't *quite* as ready as he'd thought he was to let it go—along with the memories that came with it.

When he was emptying the hallway closet a few minutes ago, he'd pulled down a blanket that MaryBeth used to cover herself with on cold winter nights. He'd held it to his nose breathing in deep, trying to catch a scent of her perfume. Instead, he inhaled dust and sneezed.

He looked at the box of donations where the blanket now sat on top. He thought they'd have forever together, and now he was packing away the rest of their items, destined for the resale store and charity. He leaned down and pushed the blanket aside so he could take one more look at their lives together. There was her favorite mug that she'd bought on their honeymoon in Hawaii. The paint had faded off of it even while she was alive, erasing two of the islands. Some of her recipe books, yellowed with age, took up space in the bottom of the box. She used to collect them, and Jesse was almost positive that she never used a few of them. He remembered her excitement at finding a candy cane cake that she'd wanted to try.

I'm going to make this for Christmas this year, she'd said. *Doesn't it look amazing?*

Yes, love. It'll be great.

She passed away before she had a chance to make it.

Even though it had been almost ten years, there were times he missed her so much he ached. It wasn't even about Oscar losing his mom—though that also killed him. MaryBeth had been born to be a mother. She'd always known how to reach their son, no matter what mood he was in.

No. Jesse missed the little things—the way she used to

hum in the shower when she'd get ready for the day. How she used to make the best butterscotch cookies he'd ever had in his life. He missed cuddling with her on the couch, watching gameshows in the room they'd painted together in soft yellow. He'd never gotten used to being alone after she'd passed. Maybe just as she had been made to be a mother, he was never made to be alone. And maybe his sister was right. It *was* time to start dating someone again.

Correction. He didn't want to date *someone*. He wanted to date Carly.

He'd made a damned fool of himself in front of her the other day, and she'd still smiled at him like he was someone worthy of her time. She had to have men falling all over themselves for the chance to have her smile at them like that. But she still said yes to a date with him.

Could he really do this? Could he date someone again? Especially someone who could be killed performing a job that she still did for a living?

He brushed the sweat off his forehead before he walked out on the front porch. He wanted to call Carly and he wanted to do it before he lost his nerve, but he couldn't do it inside MaryBeth's house. It wasn't like the ghost of her lingered and she'd curse him if she overheard him asking someone else out. She was at peace, and he'd taken comfort in that over the years. But…he still couldn't ask another woman out in her house.

Before Jesse could talk himself out of it, he hit Dial on his phone. He walked down to the patch of grass in the front yard. He started pacing to let out some nervous energy as he listened to the phone ring. What if it went to voicemail? Should he leave her a message or send her a text? Maybe he'd message Amanda directly for more advice. He didn't need to be Benjamin's entertainment for the day.

Relief rushed through him when Carly finally answered. "Hello?"

"Hey, it's Jesse. Jesse Abernathy. From the football game…and the pie." He quietly smacked himself in the forehead. Why had he mentioned the pie? She'd brought it over as an unnecessary apology. He didn't need to unintentionally guilt trip her. Would he always be a bumbling fool around this woman?

Carly let out a soft laugh, the sound turning him into liquid. "Hey, Jesse." Her voice was light and airy. He wished he could record her speaking because just the tone of her voice relaxed him in ways he couldn't explain. She paused for a second before she said, "I was wondering if I'd hear from you. You ran off pretty quickly the other day."

Jesse closed his eyes briefly, remembering how she'd given him her number and he'd hurried away immediately afterward so he could get to Oscar. Had she thought that the way he'd hurried away was a sign he wasn't interested?

"I'm sorry about that. My son—he has autism, and sometimes he can get overstimulated. I saw the signs, and I wanted to get to him before things turned ugly. I understand that that can be a lot. If you want me to lose your number, I get it."

He hadn't dated since MaryBeth died. That hadn't meant he'd been living the life of a celibate either. He'd had some pleasant enough encounters over the years, and there was one woman he'd had a standing arrangement with for a few months. She'd been the mother of one of

Oscar's classmates and a recent divorcee. They'd met at a parent-teacher conference, both waiting in line to speak with their children's teacher. They'd exchanged numbers that night, and she'd texted him the next day, explaining that she wasn't ready for a relationship but she had needs. He certainly hadn't been ready for a relationship either, his grief only a few years old at that time. They would meet up whenever her ex had their child during the weekend.

The relationship had been mutually beneficial, and Jesse enjoyed it for what it was. He hadn't developed feelings for the woman. But unfortunately, she had. They'd been in bed together one night, seeking pleasure in one another, when his phone rang. The only person who would have called him at that time was Oscar's babysitter, and he'd pulled away to answer the phone. When he'd heard that Oscar was having a bad night, he said he'd be right there. The woman hadn't been happy. She'd told him the babysitter could handle it, but he'd left anyway. She messaged him the next morning and said that she loved him but she needed to come first. He told her Oscar would always be his priority, and she'd responded by telling him to lose her number.

"Why would I not want to go out with you because your son has autism?" Carly responded after a brief pause.

Jesse winced. It was barely there, but he could pick out that he had either hurt or offended her.

He began to pace around the yard. "Sorry…it's just…it wouldn't be the first time. I've found that…some people don't want to be in my life when they hear my son is on the spectrum."

"Oh, I see." Carly's voice was tentative. "I'm not that kind of person."

Jesse grimaced. He was blowing this. "I know. I tend to be a little guarded, especially when it comes to Oscar. I'm sorry."

"I get it," she said after a moment. "Trust is a hard thing to earn, especially when so many people have broken it before." He frowned at that, wondering who broke hers to make her sound so disillusioned. But before he could ask about it, she continued, "I'm still good with going out, if you'd like."

His body loosened at that, the tension he was carrying leaving him. "Yeah, absolutely. That's great. How about this Saturday? Can I pick you up and take you to dinner?"

"I'd like that."

He fist-bumped the air. "That's awesome. Okay. Good. I—I'll see you then. Six o'clock."

"Bye, Jesse," she replied, sounding slightly amused. "I'll see you on Saturday."

He grinned. "See you on Saturday, Carly."

They disconnected the call, and Jesse looked back at the house, taking in the two-story brick colonial that had been his home for so long. Saying goodbye to this house was finally closing a significant chapter in his life. He'd taught Oscar how to ride his bike on the sidewalk. His son had taken his first steps in the living room. They'd marked his growth on the inside of the hallway door. And then there were the memories of MaryBeth…

Can you believe it? MaryBeth said as he looked at the roof that needed to be replaced, the driveway that needed to be re-cemented.

A good starter home? I'm never going to leave. She

turned to him, her long brown hair flying around her shoulders as she looked at him with those incredible green eyes—Oscar's eyes. *We're going to be so happy here! Now carry me up the threshold, husband of mine, and let's go christen every room in the house.*

He'd laughed, pushing away the unsettled feeling he'd gotten when she mentioned it being their forever home. He hadn't realized at the time how many times they'd fight over this very house—with Jesse wanting to move out to the country and MaryBeth being adamant that they stay right where they were.

He'd mourned her, holding on to his grief like a shield, but it hadn't done him or his son any good. He'd closed himself off from others, and Oscar had copied him, doing the same thing. It was why he'd moved them to Tenacity. They both needed a fresh start. He hadn't planned on dating anyone, but he wasn't about to ruin this chance with Carly now that he had one.

He took a deep breath and stepped back into the house, his emotions swirling inside him. He felt sadness at having to let this connection to MaryBeth go, but he also felt hope for the first time in ten years…thanks to Carly. He went back into the hallway to pick up the box he'd been filling. He carried it out to his truck before going back into the house to look around one more time to make sure he got everything.

He stopped when he entered the kitchen. The appliances were outdated and the cupboards needed an upgrade. He wouldn't be surprised if it was the first room the new homeowners ripped apart and renovated. Quite frankly, Jesse never really had time for this part of the house. He was a crap cook on a good day. But that wasn't the only reason he'd avoided it.

This was the room where he'd found MaryBeth that fateful day. His memories played the horrific sound of Oscar crying hysterically as the little boy paced the floor next to his unconscious mother. Jesse could almost still feel the clamminess of MaryBeth's skin when he'd hurriedly kneeled by her side and clutched her hand to his chest, screaming—pleading—with her to stay with them while the approaching ambulance wailed somewhere in the distance.

The aneurysm had been as mercilessly swift as it had been fatal.

Jesse blinked away the tears that tried to escape his eyes now. He pushed the moment out of his head, only to find himself staring at the spot on the faded yellow linoleum floor where he'd found his wife.

His hand held his phone in a grip so hard it ached. It suddenly felt like a lifeline. A connection to a second chance at happiness if he only reached for it. And maybe that was what this whole thing with Carly was. A second chance.

He squatted down next to the spot. He lifted his fingers to his mouth and kissed them before pressing them down to the floor.

Jesse whispered, "Goodbye, MaryBeth."

He stood up and exited the house, shutting the door gently behind him.

Chapter Seven

Carly stared nervously at her reflection in the mirror. She didn't know where Jesse was taking her for their first date, but she'd wanted to wow him. She stood in her robe but held a milkmaid-style red floral dress against her body. The dress was one of her favorites, and it hugged her curves in all the right places. Carly resisted the urge to grab her matching Stetson and shove it onto her boundless hair. It sat on her dresser, a familiar armor she'd worn through rodeos and heartbreaks, protecting her against unwanted eyes. Whenever she wore it, she felt like the strong, no-nonsense woman that she was supposed to be. But she wasn't going for that image tonight. She wanted a soft, approachable, come-hither look.

As she hung the dress on her closet door handle so she could start putting her makeup on, she heard her phone ring. Her mood immediately took a dive. When Jesse hadn't called her for days after they'd run into each other at the game, Carly had assumed he wasn't interested in her after all. It had disappointed her, more than it should have. She was almost embarrassed with how many times she'd checked her phone before he'd called, always feeling let down when there was no message or missed call from him. She'd wanted to message him, but she'd stupidly only given him her number. He had never given his in return.

By the fourth day, she'd pretty much given up. She'd tried not to let it affect her mood too much. She had other things to focus on.

Carly had spent the week researching what she needed to do to get her school off the ground. She still hadn't decided if she was going to pursue it or not, but it didn't hurt to start a business plan. Just in case she needed to apply for any grants or loans.

That hadn't stopped a little pit from forming in her stomach whenever her phone remained silent, leaving her with a deflated sensation. She felt like she'd missed out on something that she hadn't even realized she had. It was unsettling.

By the fourth day of zero communication from Jesse, Carly had convinced herself that she'd imagined his interest. When he finally did call, she'd actually been taken aback. She had wanted to give him a hard time about it when she'd heard his voice, but there had been something in his tone. He'd sounded a little sad, and despite her mood, she hadn't hesitated to say yes.

Jesse Abernathy fascinated her. He was like no one she'd ever met. Her last boyfriend, Fletch, was similar to her, someone who lived for the circuit life. He had loved the limelight—and the groupies—a little too much. It had actually been a relief to see the man go. Neither of them had expected to be each other's forevers, but she had foolishly expected him to be faithful. Especially after they'd become Australia's it couple, thanks to Fletch's family connections. His father owned one of the top PR firms in the world—just one of his many business ventures—

and Fletch had made sure they were always in the spotlight. Carly had grown burned out on that life, even if it had put her on a level where money poured in faster than she could spend it.

Jesse was the complete opposite of Fletch. He was almost shy around her, and she found it refreshing. He didn't seem to care that she was a well-known person in her industry. She was pretty sure he didn't even realize how famous she was. He hadn't even known *who* she was until his son had said something. Most of the men in her circle had loved what she could bring to them by dating her. Fame, building their ego. To date someone who couldn't care less that her last show had sold out in eight hours was really refreshing. She had really looked forward to his call, which was why she'd felt more than a little crushed when he hadn't made the effort.

And if he was calling her now to cancel their date, she either was going to track the man down and give him a good talking to…or buy herself the biggest tub of ice cream she could find and eat her sorrows away for the rest of the night.

She hurried to get the phone, answering it without looking at the caller ID. "Hello?"

"Carly, my girl, how are you?"

She frowned. It took her a second to realize that it was her agent calling and not Jesse. Her emotions went from dread to joy to caution in the span of a second. "Oh! Hello, Dex. I'm doing good. Sorry—I wasn't expecting you to call."

"I know, I know. You're on a break. But I have some exciting news!"

"Okay," Carly replied, her stomach suddenly tensing

with nerves. The last time he'd had exciting news, she'd ended up in Australia for years.

"I've been in contact with a company in Europe," he said quickly, as though already sensing the direction of her thoughts. "They're starting a tour in a couple of months, and they want to give you top billing. This is what we've been waiting for. This will knock you out of the park. Sponsors are already salivating at the idea of you joining the circuit. And that's not even talking about the pay they want to offer you."

He named a number that made her head spin. Carly was already well off, but the amount Dex mentioned would mean that she would never have to worry about money again.

"What do you say? Should I have them draw up the contract?" Dex asked.

"I..." She knew she should say yes. A part of her was cursing the other half for even hesitating, and yet she found herself saying, "Can I think about it?"

"Think about it? What is there to think about? Girlie, this is the chance of a lifetime. It'll set you apart from all of the other rodeo riders out there."

"I know, and I appreciate you telling me about it, but I told you before—I'm exhausted. I've only been home for a few weeks, Dex, and I have Remi's wedding coming up, and Amy's daughter will be turning one soon. Plus, I bought myself this homestead, and I don't know if I want to leave it before I can get any work done on it."

Then there was Jesse. Not that Carly would ever make a life-altering decision based on a man, especially one she barely knew, but she couldn't help but think of her earlier excitement when he'd called her. How flattered she'd been when he stumbled his way through asking her out. Yes, the rodeo tour would put her in the stratosphere, but did she need that anymore when there were possible other options for her, just like her mother said.

"I still need to think about it," she told Dex.

He sighed, long and dramatic. "Sure, sure. You think about it. But let me know soon, all right?"

"I will." They hung up, but Carly could tell from Dex's tone that he fully expected her to accept.

A knock on the door made her frown. She still had an hour before Jesse was supposed to be here. She grimaced down at her silk robe but ran to answer the door.

"Oh, thank goodness," she said when she saw Amy and Remi. She would have been mortified if it'd been her date. "Wait…what are you doing here?"

"We're here to make sure you look your hottest," Amy said as she stepped in Carly's house, followed by Remi.

"Let's start with wardrobe," Remi said as they each grabbed one of her arms and dragged her into her room. "What are you wearing?"

"I thought this with my black-and-red cowgirl boots," Carly answered, waving her hand at her dress.

"Okay, perfect," Amy said. "That'll have him thirsting over you for sure."

"I'll grab the makeup while you work on the hair," Remi told Amy.

"I can do my own hair and makeup, you know," Carly said. But her sister and cousin shushed her as they pulled her into the en suite bathroom. They pushed her into the chair in front of her bathroom vanity and began to work.

"Are you excited?" Remi asked as she applied foundation. "Or do you feel like you want to throw up? First dates are always nerve-wracking."

"Honestly?" she said. "A little bit of both."

Amy grabbed her curling iron and plugged it in. As she waited for it to warm, she eyed her sister critically. "You *do* look more queasy than excited."

Carly waved off her concern. She really wished she'd hit Ignore on Dex's call.

Amy's eyes narrowed on her sister as she grabbed a lock of her hair and got to work. "Your energy is off. What's up?"

Carly sighed. Her family always knew how to read her like a book. "Dex called before you arrived..."

She explained the offer that the European company had given her.

Amy finished with the curling iron and grabbed a bobby pin and started to secure her hair in a loose updo. "Are you going to take it?"

"I don't know. I told him I wanted to think about it. I just got to Tenacity. I feel like I haven't even had a chance to breathe yet. I'm not sure if I want to get back on the road so soon."

"You'll do what's best," Remi assured her. "You always do."

"Yeah," Amy said, but her face was sad. Carly's anxiety over the decision she knew she'd have to make grew at that look. She had an idea what her sister was thinking. They had just reunited, and now Carly might move away again for who knew how long.

"Well, worry about that another day," Remi said. She grabbed Carly's dress where it was hanging and helped her into it. When they were done, Amy and Remi stepped back, looking her over with matching satisfied expressions.

"I think our work here is done," Amy said.

Remi nodded. "I agree." She pointed toward the mirror with her chin. "Well, what do you think?"

Carly turned to look and almost gasped. Despite her worries, her family had done wonders to her. The dress still fit to perfection, but Remi's handy makeup work made Carly's face practically glow. Amy had clasped her hair into a twist that gathered at the top, spilling over in curls. She felt beautiful.

"Thank you both," she said, hugging one then the other.

"Let us know how the date goes," Amy instructed as they headed toward the door.

"In disgusting detail," Remi added.

Carly let out a laugh before giving her cousin a light shove. "Would you get out of here?"

They had barely driven out of the driveway when a pickup truck pulled in. Carly's heart leapt in her throat when she realized that the driver was Jesse.

She didn't know what the future was going to bring, but maybe tonight would give her some direction.

Chapter Eight

Jesse's mouth dropped when Carly stepped out of her house. She looked like a goddess.

"You're beautiful," he whispered before clearing his voice. "I mean—you look beautiful."

She smiled so brightly, his chest tightened at the sight of it.

"Thank you," she responded.

As she came down her steps, he put his hand on the small of her back, enjoying the heat of her. She smelled so good—like fresh rain and apples. He was half-tempted to bury his face against her neck to see if the scent was coming from there or the fragile-looking curls of her hair.

He guided her to his pale blue truck and opened the door for her. Once she was settled, Jesse hurried around the front of the car and hopped in.

"You look really good yourself," Carly said as he started the engine.

He gave her a sheepish grin. "Thanks. My son helped me pick out the shirt."

He ran a hand over the tiny checkered blue-and-gray button-down. He and Oscar had spent a good hour going through his closet. Oscar encouraged him to ditch the usual flannel and cowboy hat so that he could look the part of someone who wanted to "actually date someone who's a baddie."

He didn't know where his son came up with this stuff half the time. Though…he wasn't wrong. He did want to date Carly. Badly.

Carly gave a light laugh as she buckled herself in. "My sister and cousin came over to help me get ready. I don't know how I made it so many years in Australia without their help."

He didn't miss the wistful sound in her voice. "Do you miss it? Australia?" he asked as he pulled onto the road. His stomach tightened. He'd been wondering if she had any longing to return to that life, and he held his breath as he awaited her answer.

Carly was thoughtful for a moment. "It's a beautiful country. A gorgeous mix between wilderness and suburbia. I made a lot of good friends while I was there and I miss them, but being on the road all the time gets exhausting. And things were getting a little hectic toward the end of my tour there. I used to live for the rush of performing, but… I've been looking forward to taking some time off to enjoy the peace and quiet. Plus, there's a lot of appeal to staying put instead of endlessly living out of a suitcase."

She frowned for a second as though a memory popped up that she didn't like. She turned her head away from him to stare out the window. He wanted to ask her more about what she said. He was curious what had made her life so hectic, but given her body language, he decided not to pursue it.

"I think I understand what you mean," Jesse finally said, while relief coursed through him. It didn't sound like she planned on leaving anytime soon. "I grew up on a ranch and missed the lifestyle when I lived in Houston."

"How long did you live there?" Carly asked.

"Eighteen years," he answered.

He'd met MaryBeth by chance. He'd been in town for his friend's engagement party. On his way home, he'd stopped into a coffee shop to get some much-needed caffeine for the road. MaryBeth had been there, sitting by the window, drinking one of those sugary drinks she favored, while reading a book. He'd stopped dead in his tracks when he'd spotted her. He sat down at the table beside her and asked about her book. She'd looked up, irritation on her face at being interrupted, but it quickly dissipated when she met his eyes. They were married six months later.

Carly returned her gaze to his face. "What made you decide to move to Tenacity after being in the city for so long?"

"My son was a big factor. He seemed so unhappy in the school he was in. It's hard for him to make friends, even though I know he desperately wants them. When we visited Tenacity and we both loved it, I decided it was time for a fresh start. For both of us."

He didn't elaborate. It felt weird to bring up MaryBeth or the fact that this was his first real date in ten years. It was still hard for him to talk about what happened to his family that day. Plus how many dating partners wanted to hear about your dead spouse?

Thankfully, they soon reached Castillo's Mexican Restaurant, which JenniLynn had recommended.

"I hope you like Mexican food," he said, a little nervous. He was going for a romantic atmosphere tonight, but not overly so. Jesse wanted to be able to talk to this woman, not shout at one another over music like at the Grizzly Bar. But if she wasn't a fan of the food, he'd have to scramble for another idea.

"I love it," she replied, much to Jesse's relief.

They entered the restaurant, and his tension lessened even further. The place was small and cozy, if a little dark, but the candlelight on the tables helped with that. The seating area had small windows that overlooked the street. There were wooden booths placed throughout the space and a small bar in the back took up the remaining dining area.

A woman in her sixties approached. "Welcome. Is it just the two of you tonight?"

"Yes," Jesse said.

"Wonderful, right this way." The hostess led them to a corner table. They passed by several patrons who either waved, nodded at them, or started whispering among one another.

"Is this your first time here?" the hostess asked.

"Yes," Carly replied, while Jesse nodded.

"I'm Yolanda," the woman said. "My husband and I have proudly owned Castillo's for over thirty years now, and our sons work here now too." Yolanda pointed to the table where there were already menus waiting. "I'll give you a few minutes to look over what we have to offer."

"Thank you," Jesse replied.

"This all sounds amazing," Carly said as she looked over the menu. "I haven't had authentic Mexican food in so long."

Jesse cocked his head. "They don't have Mexican restaurants in Australia?"

"They do, but I didn't get to really enjoy life there. It was mostly work."

"How long were you there for?" he asked.

"About ten years," Carly replied, her eyes skimming over the quesadilla section. "Oh, the cheese quesadillas sound good."

Jesses's eyebrows shot up. "Ten years and you didn't get to enjoy any Mexican food? No one took you on a date for some?"

He was fishing, and she smirked like she knew it too.

"There was one man I dated for a while, but we were both on the circuit. I was too busy winning, and he was too busy flirting with groupies."

Carly said it lightly, as if it was a joke, but he sensed the hurt under the bravado.

"I'm sorry," he replied just as Yolanda returned with waters and took their order.

After she left, Carly placed her arms on the table. "What about you? Are Mexican restaurants your normal go-to when you date someone?"

"No… I…" Jesse didn't want to talk about it, but he might as well rip the Band-Aid off. "I haven't really dated anyone since my wife died."

The amusement on her face disappeared instantly. "I'm so sorry. I didn't know."

Jesse shrugged. "I don't really talk about it."

Carly picked up her water and took a sip before she tactfully changed the subject. "What about Oscar? How's he doing with the move?"

Jesse appreciated the deliberate effort that she'd made to get them out of a sticky conversation. "He seems better. School's hard for him. He doesn't exactly understand social cues. If someone is mad or making fun of him, he doesn't understand it and then gets upset. But I'm proud of him for joining the football team and trying to be involved. Coach Finn has taken him under his wing, which I'm grateful for. The friends might not be coming like I'd hoped they would, but he's at least talking more. I think it also helps that we're currently staying with Grayson and JenniLynn. Her youngest is on the spectrum, so they're both great at reading when Oscar's having a bad day."

He ran a hand over the slight whiskers on his jaw. "It's good to be around family. I've felt really alone trying to raise Oscar without having a support system nearby. MaryBeth—my late wife—she was a great mother and always knew how to make sure Oscar had everything he needed, mentally and emotionally. Sometimes I feel like I'm failing him."

Carly reached over and squeezed his hand. "I don't know Oscar well, considering that I just met him the one time, but I didn't get the impression that he was failing at life. He seemed like a happy teenage boy."

She went to withdraw her palm, but Jesse's free hand grabbed hers and held it against his other one.

"Thank you," he said softly.

"You're welcome," she returned with a small smile. In that moment with the soft candlelight from the table flickering over her features Carly looked so beautiful that Jesse would have been happy sitting there looking at her all night.

The moment was broken up by Yolanda returning to the table, delivering a mango margarita for Carly and a beer for him.

"What about you?" Jesse asked after taking a sip of his beer. "How are you settling into life in Tenacity?"

She sat back in her chair as she considered his question. "It's definitely been a change of pace, that's for sure. But it's good. Lots of people still stop and whisper—" She tilted her head toward a couple looking their way. They quickly turned their attention back to the table in front of them. "But people aren't rude when they recognize me. Some people can be really assertive toward me and my sisters because of our careers. Not to mention the press. It's a nice change of pace to be in a place where most people's concerns are what color you're painting your barn instead of what race you've won or who you're dating."

"Oh, I don't know about that," Jesse joked. "JenniLynn said the social network in town was buzzing after I said hi to you at the football game."

Carly let out a startled giggle at the realization, and Jesse basked in the sound of it.

"I can't imagine being on the rodeo circuit," he said. "What's it like? Other than people wanting a piece of you."

"Busy," she replied. "It's not just about loading up your horse and getting to your next stop. It's a business like everything else. I have an agent and publicist. There are nonstop meetings with sponsors and event organizers. I loved it for so long. To be honest, it's been all I've known since I was adopted." She licked at the salt on her margarita glass, and he became transfixed at the trail of her tongue along the glass. "But I've been excited for the change."

He didn't miss the way her face dimmed, similar to how she looked in the car when she touched on the subject earlier. He frowned, wondering about that expression. He wanted to peel away the layers she seemed to be burying herself under so he could see what she was thinking and why she looked so cautious all of a sudden.

Yolanda returned again, this time with their food.

"This smells so good," Carly told the woman.

"*Gracias*," Yolanda replied. "Let me know if you need anything else."

They took a few bites of their food before Jesse said, "Your homestead is beautiful. I looked at the property myself when I was considering the move back to the area, but it sold quickly after I saw it. Your doing, I take it." He grinned at her, and she lifted her glass in mock salute.

"Sorry," Carly said. She put a dab of sour cream on top of her quesadilla and ate some more, a satisfied smile popping on her lips. "This is delicious."

A tiny bit of sour cream was left over at the corner of her mouth, and he resisted the urge to lean over and lick it off. Instead, he focused on cutting into his burrito.

"Do you have any plans for your property?" he asked after a few minutes.

Please don't say anything rodeo, please don't say anything rodeo.

Jesse knew it was Carly's career, but he hated the idea that she would go back to a job where she'd been injured multiple times.

"Well..." Carly's eyes sparkled in the candlelight. He found it hard to look away. "It's a bit of a pipe dream."

"Tell me," he said. He wanted to know everything about this woman. Her ambitions, her long-term goals. All of it.

Carly wiped at her mouth, and the taunting sour cream disappeared. "I... I want to open a horse-riding school for foster kids. I was in the system, and it was one of the worst times of my life. I'm thankful every day that I was adopted out. Others aren't so fortunate."

Jesse's heart turned a little. This woman was incredible.

"That's an amazing dream to have and one worthy of pursuing," he said. "You said earlier that you were adopted…"

"Yes. My parents were killed in an accident when I was five. I didn't have any relatives on either side of the family that wanted to take me, and I ended up in foster care for a few years."

"I'm so sorry," Jesse replied, his face etched with regret. "I shouldn't have asked."

"It's okay." Carly gave him a gentle smile. "I'm over it now, but as a kid I wasn't in a good place for a long time. I was bounced from home to home. Some places were decent. Other places…weren't. By the time I was eight, I was angry with the world. I missed my parents like crazy. I'd lost everything over the years, even the few mementos I'd had from my earliest childhood. I had a teddy bear that I absolutely loved named Oatmeal. One of the biological kids took it in one of my foster homes, and when I demanded it back because it was mine, my foster dad called me a liar and locked me in a closet for the night." She frowned, lost in the memory.

Jesse fought the urge to beg for the name of the SOB, so he could track the man down and make him suffer as he'd made Carly. But she pulled herself out of her sad thoughts and gave a self-conscious turn of the lips.

"I started acting out a lot, which caused me to be in even more homes. And then one day, I landed in the home of Suzie Hawkins and her husband, Arthur. They had already adopted my sisters by the time I came along. I made it very easy for them to hate me, but they never did. They didn't give up on me. They introduced me to horses." She laughed. "I was terrified the first time I was on one, but there was also a freedom to it that I hadn't known. Before I knew it, I was following Suzie and Arthur all over their property, practically living in their stables, and for the first time in a very long time, I started to feel safe. I didn't trust them, mind you. I'd learned early on how easy things could get taken away, and I thought they'd be taken away too."

He could see the emotion flitter across her eyes before she continued.

"Then on my tenth birthday, they officially adopted me and I took Suzie's last name. It was the best day of my life." She smiled at him, though it didn't quite reach her eyes. "Everything turned out for the best in the end. Suzie and Arthur loved me and my sisters. They took us all in and gave us a chance. It didn't matter where we came from or what problems we brought with us, they gave us back our lives. That's what I want to do with my riding school. I want to rescue horses that are bound for the slaughterhouse and unite them with kids who are also feeling lost in the world."

Tenderness spread over Jesse. Carly was truly amazing. He'd heard a lot of horror stories over the years about kids in the system, but she'd not only survived it, she became the strong, extraordinary woman who sat across from him today. And after everything she'd been through, she still wanted to give back, to give kids some hope when they might not have any left. He suddenly had a vision of a future with her, Oscar…maybe even a few adopted kids of their own.

Jesse quickly grabbed another sip of his beer. He was getting *way* too ahead of himself.

She shifted in her chair. "Wow…that's a lot to unload on a first date. Sorry about that. I think the margarita's making my tongue a little loose."

He shook his head. "I'm glad you told me, and I'm happy you got the property instead of me."

She threw back her head and laughed. Maybe he imagined it, but he thought he saw a flash of relief in her eyes when she looked at him again. He wondered how open she'd been with other men about her past, if they'd judged her for some reason. They were fools if they had.

Time flew much more quickly than Jesse ever could have wanted, and before he knew it, they were driving back to her home, still talking as they went.

As he walked Carly to her porch, she said, "I had a really good time tonight."

He mentally did a victory dance. "I'm glad to hear it since I'm out of practice."

She stepped up onto the porch stairs and turned to face him. The moonlight cascaded through the curls on her head, turning her dark brown hair to honey-dipped gold.

"You have any tips on how I can improve?" He meant to say it lightly, instead it came out low and rough.

"No notes from me. I give you an A plus," she joked with a sensual turn of her lips. He wanted to kiss her badly.

"I want to see you again," he blurted, inwardly cringing. "I mean…can I see you again?"

She didn't hold back her grin as she said, "I'd like that very much."

He glanced down at her mouth again. He wanted to feel it. Needed to.

But did women want to kiss someone on the first date these days? Should he try?

Dammit! He should have asked Grayson this before he left.

"I…" he started to say before he stepped away. "I'll call you. Good night."

He didn't look back, but he heard her murmur, "Good night?"

She sounded as confused as he felt.

Chapter Nine

Carly stood in line inside the finance office at Tenacity Town Hall. As she waited for her turn, she tried to talk herself out of wasting her time. There was no point of even putting in an application until she knew that she was going to move forward with her riding school. But even as she told herself this, she couldn't get her feet to move. She didn't know how long it would take to get a business application, but she wanted to get the ball rolling...just in case.

"Next," a woman called out. She wore a button-up blue cardigan, and her white hair was in a tight bun on top of her head. The nameplate on the counter in front of her said *Dorothy*.

"Hello, I'm Carly H—"

"Hawkins, yes, I know, dear." The older woman looked at her over the bridge of her glasses.

Carly's forehead wrinkled. "I'm so sorry—have we met?"

Dorothy half chuckled. "Welcome to Tenacity. Eventually you'll know everyone's name."

Another woman walked over and stood next to Dorothy. She had short brown hair, a beak-like nose, and a sour expression on her face.

"Barbara Jean and Burt said they saw you and Jesse

Abernathy at Castillo's last weekend," the new woman said. "Is that true?"

"I..." Carly was honestly shocked. She'd come in to inquire about a business application, not to get interrogated about her love life.

"Oh, Kathy, go fix your makeup," Dorothy said.

The other woman flushed before stomping away.

Dorothy shook her head. "Sorry about that. Mr. Abernathy has captured more than one woman's admiration since he and his son moved to town. Not that Kathy would ever have a shot. She has the manners of an alley cat. She used to be the manager here until she told one of our employees to come into work while the poor girl's mother was on her deathbed."

Carly didn't know how to respond to any of this. She really wasn't one for gossip or getting into fights with women over men, though she had little patience for bullies. She decided to take the higher road and mind her own business.

"I'm here to get some information regarding a business permit," she finally said.

A half hour later, Carly walked out the doors of town hall with the permits in her purse. She had anticipated it'd take months to get approval, but after she'd explained her idea to Dorothy, the woman stamped the paperwork, then asked her to pose for selfies. She hated using her name and connections for anything, but she wasn't going to say no in these circumstances either.

Now she just needed to build her business, starting with some repairs. Amy had told her about a couple of stores in the area that carried what she was looking for. Carly was in the middle of debating with herself whether she should drive or walk to the Tenacity Feed and Seed when her phone thrummed inside her pants pocket. She glanced at her watch to see who was calling.

Dex. Again.

She hit Ignore like she had every time her agent had called. She knew she needed to give him an answer soon, but weren't the permits answer enough? Granted, she could do the European tour, come back, and work on her school after that. The money would certainly help make sure that her business had no way of failing.

But…

She needed more time. Just the thought of going back on the road made her stomach turn. Besides wanting the mental reset, there were other things to consider. Honestly, the idea of her riding school was very appealing because it would be *hers*. As she'd mentioned to Jesse during their date, she'd lost most of her belongings being bounced from house to house during her time in foster care. Even though her adoptive family made sure she lacked for nothing, there was a lot of appeal to bringing her dream to fruition. It was something other than being one of the Hawkins Sisters.

Not that she was ashamed or ungrateful for the legacy that she had with her family. But was it wrong to want to have something for herself? More importantly, it'd be something that could really help a kid who was feeling as desperate and lonely as she had once been.

As Carly walked down the steps, her mind went back to her conversation with Jesse. That date had been one of the best ones she had ever been on. It wasn't anything outrageous. Her ex's idea of a date was to go skydiving or do something that would surely get the paparazzi's attention.

Her date with Jesse had been just about them. No cameras. No one coming up to take her picture. Sure, there had been plenty of whispers and eyes on them, and gossip was apparently swirling about the two of them, but that seemed to be the way of Tenacity. Small towns had a tendency to know everyone's business.

She'd told him about her past—more than she'd ever shared with any man before, including Fletch—and Jesse had opened up about his wife. She thought they'd had a connection.

When he'd walked her to her front porch, her heart had been hammering almost out of her chest. The way that he looked at her had made her want to *swoon*. She had practically puckered up her lips in anticipation of his kiss. Instead, he'd hightailed it out of there so fast, she'd cupped her hand over her mouth for a quick breath check to make sure it wasn't offensive.

Carly hadn't heard from him in the week since. So she was more than a little surprised when she glanced across the street and saw the man in the flesh. She stumbled to a stop. Had she manifested him? Jesse was stepping out of the Silver Spur Café, his son following behind him. He didn't notice her at first as he adjusted his beige cowboy hat on his head.

Oscar saw her and started waving excitedly in her direction. Jesse turned his head to see who his son was looking at and finally spotted her. His face immediately lit up, which softened some of the hurt she was feeling about him ghosting her. He said something to Oscar, and they both crossed the road to reach her.

"Hey," he said, his blue eyes looking like jewels in the afternoon light.

"Hi," she responded. She turned her attention to the teen by his side. "Hi, Oscar. How are you?"

"Good," he responded. "What were you doing at the town hall?"

"Oscar, that's not really our business," Jesse told his son, whose excited face lost some enthusiasm.

"It's fine," Carly said. "I was getting permits for the school I want to open."

"What kind of school?" Oscar asked. When she gave him a brief overview of what she wanted to do, the teenager became even more animated. "I want to help. Can I work for you? I can clean out the stables and feed the horses."

Jesse frowned. "That's a big responsibility, bud."

"I can do it," Oscar snapped at his dad, his hands starting to clench and unclench at his sides.

"I'd be happy to think about it," Carly said as a way to keep the peace. "First, I need to rebuild parts of the homestead before I can even think about hiring help. I was actually on my way to the feed and seed store to get some pricing on fencing."

"We were headed that way ourselves," Jesse said. "We need to get some pipes for our new bathroom. Can we walk you there?"

"Sure," she replied. They headed toward the store. The silence between father and son was palpable. "So, um, how was your lunch?" she said to break the tension.

"It was great," Jesse said. "We were planning on getting some pie from the bakery later. I have to introduce Oscar to their apple pie. I think I might have gotten a little addicted to it."

He gave her a stiff smile while keeping an eye on

Oscar, who was now tightening his hands so hard it looked like it hurt. After Jesse had asked her out, she had done some research on autism. She wondered if tightening his fists was one of the teen's stims.

"Oscar," Carly said, "if you had to choose between Nieve and a horse like Secretariat, who would you choose?"

Oscar paused his hand movement and his face lost some of its tension. "They were used for two different sports. It's not a fair comparison."

"But if you had to choose…which one would you want in your stable?"

It was enough to get Oscar to stop the painful gripping. "Well, if you compare them side by side…"

He then proceeded to tell them about the positives and negatives of each horse until they reached the store.

"While I have to agree with you that it's a bit unfair to compare any horse to Secretariat," Carly said as they entered the building, "I have to admit I'm partial to Nieve."

Oscar paused, his face thoughtful before he said, "Me too."

"Well… I should—" she started to say, ready to leave them to it, when Oscar spoke up again.

"I'm going to go look at the baby chickens." He then stomped off, clearly still annoyed with his dad.

If she was honest with herself, that made two of them. Carly wanted to ask Jesse why he hadn't called or even bothered texting her after their date. But he already looked upset as he watched his son walk away. No need to kick the man when he was already down.

Jesse sighed before turning to Carly and asking, "Want some company?"

"Okay," she replied.

"Thank you, by the way," Jesse said as they walked toward the lumber part of the store.

"For what?" she asked.

"For pulling Oscar out of hurting himself. You're really good with him."

"It was nothing," she said right as a salesperson came up to them. The tag on his shirt read the name, Mel. He seemed to be expecting her.

That was confirmed when he said, "Dorothy called me and said you might be on your way over."

Her eyebrows pulled together till she remembered that she'd mentioned in passing that she wanted to get some pricing on wood. Dorothy had recommended she check out Tenacity Feed and Seed, which was one of the ones Amy had also mentioned to her.

"I wanted to get a quote for lumber that I need for my paddock." She told him the measurements, and after he worked up some numbers, she put in an order and arranged for the delivery date. In the meantime, she bought some wood to repair a part of her barn. The salesman said he'd have the smaller purchase ready and waiting in the front of the store.

"So you're really doing it," Jesse said as they walked toward the plumbing area. "You're going to turn your dream into a reality?"

"I'm going to try," Carly responded. She didn't know when she'd officially open the school, whether it would be anytime soon or years down the road, but she could at least get things fixed on her property in preparation.

She watched Jesse sort through the different pipes until he found what he was looking for. She didn't know why she was waiting with him. She hadn't needed his help, and he didn't need hers. But Carly was reluctant to leave. Not until she had answers.

"Can I ask you something?" she asked.

"Sure," he said.

"I thought we had a good time the other night."

Jesse stopped looking at another pipe, his gaze shooting to hers. "We did. Didn't we?"

Carly folded her arms over her chest. "You tell me. You said you had a nice time and that you wanted to date me more, and then…nothing. I haven't heard from you since."

Jesse closed his eyes briefly. "I'm sorry. I told you I was out of practice." He looked toward the area where they sold baby chickens and spotted Oscar. "Oscar had a bit of a tough week at school. He came home upset because of some stuff with the football team. Finn and I worked things out with him, but it's taken up more of my time than I anticipated. Not that it's any excuse. I should have at least texted you. I'm sorry."

Carly's demeanor melted a little despite wanting to stay mad. "I get that your son needs to be your priority. I wouldn't want to go out with you if you didn't put him first. But an occasional text would be nice."

"I'll do better, I promise." Jesse used the hand not carrying the pipes and traced an *X* over his chest.

Carly smiled despite herself. "Fine. You're forgiven."

"I believe we did discuss another date last time I saw you."

Carly tapped her finger against her chin. "Is that right?"

"Even though this is very last minute and you have

every right to say no, are you free tonight? I'd love to take you to a place that my future sister-in-law told me about."

She had absolutely zero plans that night other than to sit on her couch and watch reruns. Spending more time with Jesse seemed a much better option.

"I think I can do that."

"Good," Jesse replied. Oscar noticed them and reluctantly rejoined his father. They made their way up to the cash register. Carly stopped when she saw the large slab of wood she ordered. There was no way she was going to be able to fit that in her car.

"What's wrong?" Jesse asked.

"I think I bit off more than I can chew," she replied, waving at the board. "Big board. Small car." She shrugged.

"We can take it for you," he offered. "We can throw it in the back of my truck."

"Oh, I don't want to impose."

"You live right near us," Jesse said. "It wouldn't be a problem."

Which was how Carly found herself pulling into her driveway a short time later with Jesse and Oscar following in their truck after a quick stop to the bakery. They pulled up to the barn, and Carly got out of her car.

"Where do you want this?" Jesse said as he nodded toward the wooden board sticking out of the cab of his truck.

"Against the barn is fine," she told him. She walked over to help them, but Jesse shooed her away.

"We've got this," he told her.

"My macho man," she joked. She was more than capable of helping with the heavy lumber, even if there was a tiny part of her that liked seeing Jesse's arms strain inside his shirt as he and Oscar lifted the board and brought it to where she stood. They placed it where she requested.

Oscar was still upset with his dad, given the way he was coldly looking at him.

He turned to her and said, "Can I see your horse?"

"Oscar..." Jesse said.

"I can't even look at a horse now?" Oscar retorted.

"You can look at him," Carly replied. "Just be careful. Nieve can be a bit temperamental when he's in a mood."

Oscar brushed by his father without another word. Jesse watched him go before rubbing his forehead. "Is he okay with your horse if Nieve doesn't do well around people?"

"I didn't say that Nieve wasn't good with people. He's used to being around large crowds and little kids running up to him. That said, he's one of the biggest divas in the world, which is why I said he's temperamental."

"Sorry," Jesse muttered. He looked lost for a moment. "Like I told you the other day, my wife was always better at dealing with Oscar than me. I seem to tick him off all the time."

Carly bit her lip before saying, "Maybe it wouldn't hurt to give him some space."

Jesse stiffened at that. "He needs someone to look out for him."

"And you can do that, but...he's a teenager. He's clearly trying to figure out his own way. It's hard to do that when someone is constantly looking out for you and not letting you make your own choices."

A muscle in Jesse's jaw ticked. "I don't want him to get hurt."

"I get it, but unfortunately, that's life, right? You make mistakes, you get hurt, and you grow." Carly glanced toward Oscar to make sure that Nieve was being good for him. Oscar was leaning against the wall opposite the horse's stall. He was talking to the white stallion, but it was low enough that neither she nor Jesse could hear what he was saying.

Jesse rubbed at his forehead again. "You're right. I need to let him grow up and loosen the reins a little bit."

She shook her head. "You know what? I don't know what I'm talking about. He's your son. You need to do what's best for him."

"No, I've been overly protective of Oscar. It's not helping him to have me hover over him like a worried hen."

She started to open her mouth to apologize when she noticed the streak of grime on his forehead. "Um," Carly started with a smile, "you have some dirt or something on your forehead."

"What?" Jesse looked down at his hands. They were filthy from moving the board. "Crap."

"There's a sink in my tack room if you want to wash your hands," Carly told him.

"Yeah, thanks." He looked over at Oscar, and Carly lifted a brow. He noticed the look and said, "I know, I know…give him space."

Carly let out a small laugh. She watched Jesse disappear inside the room she'd indicated. She was relieved that he wasn't upset that she stuck her nose into his business. Carly had never been good at keeping her opinions to herself, especially when she saw something that didn't sit right with her.

She glanced into the barn again and saw Oscar now

running his hand down Nieve's forehead. The giant horse nuzzled his nose against the boy's chest. Carly's eyebrows raised at the interaction. While Nieve was typically good around people he didn't know, he didn't exactly cuddle with anyone but her.

"You're really good with him," Carly said as she approached Oscar and the horse.

Oscar turned his face away quickly and rubbed at his cheeks. When he turned to face her, Carly could tell he'd been crying and was doing his best to hide it from her.

"You know," she said as she reached out to pat Nieve, "I don't like to spoil him with too many sweets, but he does love the occasional sugar cube."

She reached into her pocket and pulled a couple out before handing them to Oscar. The teen placed them in his palm and held them out to the horse, who took them gently.

The corner of Oscar's mouth ticked up. "It tickles."

"He likes you. He doesn't usually warm up to people like that," she said. She hid her smile when the boy brightened a little. "We can talk more about you helping out once the program is up and running, as long as your dad agrees."

Oscar's shoulders instantly dropped. "Dad will never say yes. He thinks I'm a toddler. He treats me like one. It's bad enough that people at school treat me like I'm a freak. It'd be really nice if I wasn't treated that way at home too."

Carly wasn't sure what to say to that. "You know, I was a few years younger than you when I entered my first race."

Oscar peeked at her in interest. "I would have thought someone with your record started much younger in life."

She shook her head. "Nope. My parents brought me into their home as a foster kid when I was about eight." When Oscar looked at her funny, she explained, "I was adopted two years later. It took me awhile to trust them. Once I finally gave them a chance, they put me on a horse. It had been my first time ever on one."

"And you were immediately great, right?" Oscar asked, a tad sarcastic.

Carly laughed. "The horse took off, and I fell, screaming, to the ground. My dad rushed to me to make sure I was okay. He told me if I needed a break from trying to learn how to ride a horse, I could take one. The general rule is if you fall off a horse, you're supposed to get right back on. My mom and dad—"

Oscar rocked on his feet. "Your mom was a three-time All-Around World Champion, right?"

"That's right," Carly said. "Even though it went against the rules, she said she was fine with me walking away from the stable that day. Because no matter what it is, you'll do everything in your power to make sure your kids are safe."

Oscar stilled for a second. He finally left out a huff. "I see what you're saying."

"Oscar," Jesse said from a distance. Carly looked behind her to see him leaning against the entryway of the barn. "We should get home."

Oscar nodded. "See you later, Carly. Thanks for letting me spend time with Nieve."

"You're welcome," she replied.

Oscar brushed by Jesse, who stared at her. His lip ticked upward, and he mouthed, *Thank you.*

Carly smiled in return. She walked the Abernathy men to their truck.

Before Jesse hopped in, he said, "We're good for tonight?"

"Yes, I'd like that."

Jesse gave her a look that tugged at her heart. He tapped the rim of his hat and said, "Ms. Hawkins."

She nodded in response. "Mr. Abernathy."

As he started up the vehicle, he poked his head out the open window. "Wear something that you can move in."

Before she could get a chance to ask what he meant, he waved goodbye, and the men left.

Chapter Ten

Carly wore another dress for her next date with Jesse. This one had long sleeves and was the color of rich burgundy. She forbade her sister and cousin from coming over. As much as she loved and appreciated them, she wanted some quiet moments to herself before Jesse picked her up.

She left her hair down, only pinning it back at the sides. Jesse said to dress so she could move, and after dragging on her red cowgirl boots, she was as ready as she was going to get. That didn't stop her from running back to the mirror to eye her selection again. Carly should have asked where they were going. Was the dress too fancy? Should she have worn her hair up?

She stared nervously in front of the mirror. She was overthinking things, but she couldn't help it. She wasn't sure what this evening would bring. She honestly thought Jesse might not be interested since he went no-contact after their first date. He was sending her mixed signals. One minute he wasn't talking to her, the next he was going out of his way to help her.

A knock on the door had Carly's pulse speeding up. Taking a breath to steady her nerves, she opened the door to find Jesse waiting on the porch. He looked just as handsome as he always did, in a black-and-white checkered shirt and black jeans. He sported a black cowboy hat that shadowed his eyes in the evening sun.

"Wow," he said. "You look amazing."

"Thanks. You don't look so bad yourself," she responded.

Jesse grinned at her before placing his hand on her back—a move she was getting a little too used to. She took a subtle breath of the woodsy cologne he wore as he guided her to his truck. He smelled so good. After he shut her door for her, he rounded the truck, and they were soon on their way.

"Am I allowed to know where we're going now?" she asked.

"I thought we might try some line dancing at the Grizzly tonight."

"You know how to line dance?" she asked.

"Not really." Jesse laughed. "But how hard can it be?"

Carly snickered. "Oh, tonight is going to be so much fun."

"Should I be nervous?" he asked.

"I guess we'll find out," she joked, feeling herself relax. "How's the house coming along?"

"Good," he answered. "Grayson and I were able to get the drywall up in Oscar's room. I think we should be able to paint it soon."

"What does Oscar think about this?" Carly had to ask as she waved her hand between the two of them.

"He thinks you're already much cooler than me," Jesse said with a self-deprecating smile. "But yes, he's happy that I asked you out. He's been really supportive about it, actually. I think he likes that I have something to focus on other than him."

Carly tried not to look too pleased at that statement. "You focus on me a lot?"

"Oh, nonstop, night and day." Jesse said it as a joke, and she laughed, but the glance he gave her as they turned down Central Avenue toward the Grizzly made her wonder if she was reading him right.

"Are you ready for this?" Carly asked him as they watched people enter the Western-style saloon. The exterior had a flat roof, like most of the commercial buildings in town. The entrance had a large orange door with weather-beaten benches to either side of it and a rough facade of bricks made from natural stone. A driveway beside the building led to a small parking lot behind the bar where they found a place to park.

Jesse smirked before offering her his hand. "Let's do it."

As they headed inside, Carly took in the crowded place. The floors were wood, and there was a long bar. Next to it was a jukebox blasting classic country music. Booths ran along the wall, and on one side of the building were some people playing pool. An antler chandelier hung overhead.

Carly glanced at Jesse and snickered when she saw his eyes go wide as he watched the line dancers moving in perfect sync to the music.

"Come on," she said, offering her hand. He took it, and they made their way to the dance floor.

An hour later, Jesse had a light sheen of sweat on his cheeks as he tried to follow her moves. "How'd you get so good at this?" he asked as he stumbled over his own foot.

"My sister Elizabeth and I would go line dancing in

between shows while we toured Australia. We didn't get a break often, but when we did, we made the most of it."

It was some of her favorite memories from the circuit, spending time with her sister. Sometimes they'd go dancing with Elizabeth's husband; other times, it was just her and Elizabeth, and they would go shopping or lie on a beach somewhere and talk. It was nice, like she and her sister were taking on the world together. It was after Elizabeth's husband died and she moved back to the States that Carly got so homesick, she'd bought the property in Tenacity.

The music changed to something slow and romantic.

Jesse's mouth turned upward. "Can I have this dance, Ms. Hawkins?"

"You may, Mr. Abernathy."

She placed her hands on his shoulders, and his went to her waist. They began to sway to the melodic sound. As they moved, she was slightly aware that there were a lot of people looking in their direction. But it was white noise. Carly was too distracted by the feel of Jesse's body under her palms, the weight of his hands on her waist.

He smelled so good, like cedar and fresh hay. As Carly slowly raised her eyes to his mouth, she wondered what it would feel like to finally be against her own lips. Against other parts of her. As she finally met his eyes, he stared intently back before his own gaze dropped to her mouth. The air around them changed, becoming electric. Her breath hitched as he tightened his hands on her waist, pulling her more firmly against him until there was no space between their bodies.

Carly wanted to feel more of him. All of him. She was just about to tell him that when the music changed and a sharp honky-tonk song came on that had the crowd cheering.

Her face felt hot—whether from dancing or from fighting back the temptation to make a public exhibition of herself, she didn't know. She pulled back so suddenly, his eyebrows shot up.

"You okay?" Jesse asked.

"I, um, I need to go freshen up. Will you excuse me?"

"Sure," Jesse said. "I'll meet you at our table."

Carly nodded and hurried toward the bathroom. As soon as she was inside, she walked over to the sink and turned on the cold water. She wet a paper towel before wiping the damp cloth over her warm cheeks. The door to the bathroom opened, and a beautiful Black woman walked in.

"Oh!" the woman said. "Hello, Carly. It's good to see you again."

"Hi, Michelle. How are you?" Carly asked in response. She'd met Michelle Corey a couple of times since officially moving to Tenacity, though she didn't know her well. Michelle's brother, Shane, was engaged to Carly's cousin Remi. The couple of times she had met Michelle, though, she had liked her, and she looked forward to having a friend in town.

Michelle joined her at the sink, copying her and wetting a towel to dab at her face. "Gosh, it's hot out there."

"It's a sign that people are having a good time," Carly replied.

Michelle leaned a hip against the sink. "You and Jesse sure looked like you were having a fun time." She wiggled her eyebrows at Carly, who laughed. "I didn't realize you two were seeing each other. You make a cute couple."

"'Seeing' is an interesting word. This is only our second date. To be honest, I'm not sure if we'll end up dating or just being really good friends."

Michelle smirked. "Good friends or not, I can only hope to find a man who will look at me someday the way Jesse looks at you."

Carly flushed all over again as she remembered what it felt like on the dance floor, to be held against Jesse. "A good man is hard to find," she said, though she hoped that Jesse might be the one for her and not a friend.

Michelle completely distracted her by saying, "Oh, I totally get that…although I already found one." Her face saddened though before she muttered quietly, "Not that he feels the same way about me."

Carly looked at the woman in concern.

She wanted to ask more about it, but Michelle changed the subject. "Are you going to participate in the Fall Dinosaur Days Rodeo?"

"I…didn't even know there was one," Carly admitted.

"Oh yeah. Tenacity's Dinosaur Days Festival is a big deal around here. Lots of places get involved. My family owns Little Cowpokes Daycare Center. We're holding a kids' event during the celebration. If you want to be a part of the rodeo, I can make some calls. I'm sure the townsfolk would be tickled pink to have one of the Hawkins Sisters perform."

"Well…if you think they'd want me there, I'd be happy to be a part of it," Carly told her.

Michelle squealed. She rushed over and gave her a hug. "I'll have Remi send you the details once I know more."

"Sounds good."

Michelle beamed at her. "I should probably stop holding you up. Your man will be wondering where you are."

She gave Carly a nod and left the room. Carly turned back to the mirror as her Michelle's words echoed in her mind.

Jesse Abernathy wasn't her man.

But she was starting to really wish he was.

She returned to their table and saw Jesse drinking a glass of water.

"I got you some water," he said, nodding toward the glass next to his.

"Thanks." She sat down next to him. "This has been a lot of fun tonight."

"Yeah," Jesse replied.

"I ran into Michelle Corey in the bathroom." She told him that Michelle asked her to do the rodeo. By the time she was done, he was frowning.

"Are you going to?" Jesse asked.

"Yeah, I think so," she replied. "Michelle said the townsfolk would enjoy it."

He stared at his glass intently. "And you're up for it?"

She gave him a puzzled look. "What do you mean?"

"The first day we met, Oscar had mentioned you were recently injured. Are you sure doing a rodeo is a good idea right now?"

Carly didn't know if she should react with indignation or lean over and kiss him for caring. "I appreciate the concern, but I'm fine. I was hardly hurt. The reporters made a bigger deal about it than necessary because I'd quit the Australian circuit around that time and moved home. The injury was seriously nothing. I'm as good as new."

She melted a little at the relief on his face.

"Can I escort you to the event?" he asked.

Carly practically glowed. That didn't sound very friend-zone-like to her. So maybe they would end up being more than just friends, just as she hoped.

"Yeah," she answered. "I'd really like that."

He cracked a grin. "Good. It's a date."

On the way home, Carly couldn't stop anticipating their good-night kiss. Everything was going so well, and after their connection earlier on the dance floor, she could not be mistaking the looks he'd been giving her all evening. He wanted to kiss her just as badly as she wanted to kiss him.

Once they arrived at her house, Jesse walked her toward her porch. She glanced toward the sky and sighed contentedly.

"I don't know what it is about Tenacity," she murmured, "but the stars seem a little bit brighter here than anywhere else I've been."

They came to a stop at her steps.

"Do you have a favorite constellation?" Jesse asked, his eyes on her instead of the sky.

"Well, I'm a Virgo, so I have to give my love to that," Carly joked. "I remember when I first arrived at Suzie's place, she and Arthur took all of us to an observatory. I got to see Saturn and all its rings. You could even see their shadow against the planet. It was incredible. Before I found my forever home, I would spend hours staring up at the night sky, wishing on as many stars as I could see—which wasn't very many. Most of my foster homes were in cities, and light pollution ruined my view."

"What'd you wish for?" Jesse asked, his voice soft.

Carly's face turned a little sad. "At first, I used to wish

for my birth parents' accident to have been a mistake, that they weren't dead but were actually out searching for me. And then one night, I had a really bad night with my foster parents. The guy came home drunk and started lashing out at anything and anyone he could find. I—" She couldn't tell him what happened; she didn't want to relive it. "Anyway, later that night I went up to my room and stared up at the sky. I saw one star that night, and I wished with all my heart that I could find someone who would rescue me from the hell I was living in. When my social worker came to check on me and saw…the bruises, she removed me from the home. The next family I was sent to turned out to be Suzie and Arthur. The rest is history."

She gave him a half smile and saw that he was staring at her with sadness on his face. Oh hell, had she ruined the mood?

"I'm sorry you went through that," Jesse finally said.

Carly gave a small shrug. "It all worked out for the best in the end. I couldn't have asked for two better parents than the ones I ended up with. They introduced me to horses and the rodeo life. Everything I have is because of them." Deciding they needed a change in subject, she asked, "What about you? Any wishes on stars?"

Jesse tilted his head back and looked at the sky. "I was always too busy, I guess. When I was younger, we had my parents' ranch we had to take care of. Though sometimes my brothers and I would camp outside. We'd lay out under the night sky, and I'd count as many stars as I could before I'd fall asleep."

"I'm sure you were able to count every single one," she teased.

"I think I got to three hundred and then I'd either lose track or fall asleep," he said with a laugh.

Carly gave the stars one final look. She wished the night would never end. When she finally glanced at Jesse, she found that he was staring at her again. She could read the intention in his eyes.

"Carly…" Jesse rasped.

"Yes?" she said, trying not to sound too eager.

"I—" His phone buzzed, and Jesse dropped his gaze to the phone he pulled out from his pants pocket. He read the text, his eyes deepening in concern.

"Is everything okay?" she asked.

"Yes…just my son." He put his phone back in his pocket. "I need to go."

"Okay," Carly said, trying to hide her disappointment in the sudden ending to their date. "Thank you for the lovely evening."

"You're welcome." He stared at her for a second, his mouth opening and closing. He finally said, "Talk to you later."

"Bye," Carly responded.

She stood there for a long time, even after his truck disappeared from her view.

Chapter Eleven

Carly was in a foul mood the next day.

She liked Jesse. A lot. More than she should considering they'd only gone out a couple of times. But she really didn't understand him. One minute he looked like he felt the same way she did. The next, he was leaving like he couldn't get away from her fast enough. She understood that Oscar was his number one priority. But…he hadn't even tried to kiss her. Was he old-fashioned? Or was he just not that interested in her?

She turned down the dirt driveway of Split Valley Ranch, finally pulling to a stop in front of her sister's house. She wasn't surprised to see Amy sitting on the front porch swing in a thick sweater. Josephine slept on her lap under a thick blanket. As she got out of the car, Carly's mind replayed the previous night, the feel of being in Jesse's arms, the way she'd felt so comfortable talking about her past with him. She loved his quiet comfort. Carly appreciated that when she'd told him about the uglier sides of her childhood, he hadn't looked at her with sympathy—she wouldn't have been able to tolerate that—but he'd given her the empathy she needed. And then…she was left on her porch, watching him leave without so much as a hug or pat on the shoulder.

"Hey," Carly muttered as she climbed the steps and sat next to her sister. She shivered. She should have worn a thick coat, despite it being an unusually warm morning for late September. She made grabby hands toward Josephine, causing the porch swing to creak.

Amy snorted before handing the baby over. Josephine made a quiet mew of discontent at being moved before falling back asleep. Carly took in the perfection of her little face.

"Who's your favorite aunt?" Carly murmured as she snuggled the baby closer, breathing in her fresh baby-powder scent.

"I think Faith is," Amy joked.

"Hearsay," Carly grumbled. She kissed Josephine lightly on the head as not to disturb her. "Tori, Faith, and Elizabeth can suck it. The Best Aunt Award goes to me. I live the closest, therefore I will have more opportunities to spoil her."

"Sure, Carly," Amy replied indulgently. They rocked in the swing for several minutes before Amy said, "So you want to tell me what's wrong?"

"Who says anything is wrong?" Carly said, not meeting her sister's eyes.

"Because it's seven o'clock in the morning, and you are notorious for not being an early riser. And you looked upset when you first got out of your car. So spill."

Carly sighed. She forgot how well her family knew her. Her parents had the philosophy *sharing is caring*. They grew up speaking their minds and spewing their feelings. It was one of the reasons it took Carly awhile to get used to the Hawkins way of life. She'd always been so cautious around the people in her circle. It was a hard habit to break.

"It's Jesse," she finally said.

"Did you find out he was a bad kisser?" Amy asked, her tone light.

"I still wouldn't know," Carly mumbled.

"What! You haven't kissed him yet? Haven't you gone out a couple of times now?"

"He's probably just trying to be a gentleman," Carly halfheartedly defended.

"This isn't the 1800s, and you're both consenting adults. It's weird."

"It's not weird," Carly denied. "He's being considerate—that's all."

"Yeah, it is." Amy looked thoughtful for a minute before she carefully said, "Look, I know he has a son and everything, but…maybe he's still hung up on his former wife."

Carly huffed. "Why would he ask me out if he was?"

"I don't know. Maybe it's a case of too much emotional damage."

Carly stared at the sleeping baby in her arms, taking comfort in the weight of her.

"I don't know," she replied before admitting her deepest worry. "What if he's just not into me?"

"Then break it off and move on. There are plenty of handsome guys in town we can set you up with."

"I don't want anyone else," Carly said. "Jesse is funny and caring, and… I can honestly see myself settling down with him. He's different from all the men I've met who were either more obsessed with their careers than I am or who were only interested in hooking up with a famous Hawkins Sister. Not to mention he's a dedicated father. But..."

When she didn't continue, Amy asked "But what?"

Carly adjusted Josephine, not willing to look at her sister as she confessed, "Like you said, what if he's still hung up on his wife?" Tears filled her eyes for a second, but she quickly blinked them away. "I don't know how to compete with a ghost."

"A ghost?" Amy asked.

Carly's heart ached a little as she remembered Jesse's brief reference. "I didn't ask for details, but Jesse mentioned his *late* wife. I feel so bad that he and Oscar had to go through that type of loss."

Amy gazed at her husband in the distance. "You know, Josh and I didn't always have it smooth sailing. You have to work at a relationship and establish strong communication with one another. Maybe you need to ask for more details about his life before he moved to Tenacity. Especially how long ago it was that his wife died. I mean—Car—if she died recently..."

Carly gave a watery sigh. "I know. But when am I supposed to bring it up? We have our dates—which doesn't seem the appropriate time to ask about his dead wife."

Amy winced at that. She then said cautiously, "Maybe you should consider dating other guys." When Carly's face turned stubborn, Amy rushed, "I love you, but you do have a tendency to want to see the best in men that aren't the greatest for you. Look at your childhood crush on Paul Rodriguez."

Carly gave her a disbelieving look. "You're seriously not bringing up a boy band member that I had a crush on when I was ten."

"I'm just saying you had five boys to choose from in that group, and you became obsessed with the one who was widely known for being a player."

"He was gorgeous—still is, come to think of it! Have you watched his show, *First Comes Marriage*?"

Amy rolled her eyes in exasperation. "No, I don't have time for silly reality TV shows."

"First of all, how dare you," Carly joked. She didn't really care for that type of entertainment either, but she'd decided to check the show out one time while she was bored on the road because she'd heard Paul hosted it. She'd found herself becoming addicted to it. "If we're going to talk about this subject again, let's rehash the fact that I'm still hurt you never took me to see Holiday Boys when I was a kid, despite the fact that you could have been an awesome older sister and driven me to any of their concerts!"

"I was not subjecting my ears to a bunch of screaming preteens, thank you very much." The mirth in Amy's eyes slowly drained though as she added, "Look what happened with Fletch."

Carly scowled. "Fletch was a mistake."

"But you kept turning a blind eye to him, even when he was obviously not the one for you."

"Trust me, my eyes were wide open when it came to that man," Carly grumbled.

Josephine started to squirm before she let out a noise that indicated she needed a new diaper. Being the amazing aunt that she was, Carly handed the baby back to her sister. Amy rolled her eyes but took her daughter and stood up.

"I'm just saying," Amy continued, "don't build the

guy up too much in your head. Like you said, you don't know where his mind is at. Is he ready for a relationship, or is he still hung up on his wife to the point where he's not ready to see someone else? You don't want to end up a rebound, even if she passed years ago. Maybe the first question you need to ask him isn't about his feelings for her but if he's mentally ready for you."

Josephine let out a whine, and Amy kissed her head. "All right, my darling, let's get you changed."

Amy left Carly with nothing but thoughts she didn't want to think. She swallowed hard, knowing her sister was right. She had to guard her heart from Jesse because the last thing she needed was to fall head over heels in love with the man, only for him not to return her feelings.

She stared off in the distance where she could see Amy's husband, Josh, riding his horse as he rounded up some cattle. Carly took a breath and smelled fall leaves and hay. A breeze stirred the chimes hanging from the eaves, and for just a second, she relaxed. Her phone buzzed in her pocket, and she pulled it out to read the message. And just like that, her relaxation quickly erased. Her mouth twisted unhappily as she read another message from Dex.

The sponsors came back to me with another offer. Another $50,000!!! What are you waiting for?

Amy came back without the baby. "Your favorite niece decided she wanted a nap in the comfort of her own crib." She paused when she saw Carly staring vacantly at her phone. "What is it? What's wrong?"

Carly swallowed before showing her sister the message.

Amy read it and whistled. "You still haven't gotten back to him on that, huh?"

"I want to," Carly told her. "But every time I get my phone out to respond, my mind goes blank. I don't know how to answer. My head is screaming at me to stop being a fool and to take the offer. I know, financially, it'd be worth it."

"Well, what does your heart say?" Amy asked.

"My heart?" Carly said it like she'd never heard of the organ. She reached up her hand and pressed it against her chest where it was pounding painfully. "I… It's telling me to stay, to rest. I want to see what else life has to offer, and the idea of going back on the road again makes me feel sick."

"Here, give me your phone," Amy ordered. When Carly gave it to her with a confused look, her sister began typing rapidly. It made a swooshing noise, letting Carly know that Amy sent a message.

"What… Who did you just text?" she asked.

"Dex. I told him to stop pressuring you and if he didn't, he'd have me to deal with."

Carly cracked a smile for the first time since last night when she'd danced in Jesse's arms. Long ago, Dex had represented Amy as well. He'd never gotten away with bossing her sister around.

"Thanks," Carly said. She felt exhausted and regretted getting up so early.

Amy sat back down next to her and nudged her with her elbow. "That's what big sisters are for."

Later that day as she was leaving the barn after a nice long ride on Nieve, she felt her phone buzz in her pocket.

She pulled it out of her jacket and looked at the text. Jesse had sent her a picture of two constellations. Her brow furrowed for second, and then a flutter of warmth bloomed inside her.

Perseus and Andromeda, whose love story was forever remembered in the night sky.

Three dots appeared before another text from Jesse popped up.

These two are my favorite.

Did he know what they meant? He had to. Carly smiled, her earlier trepidation easing.

Despite Amy's advice, Carly's head was spinning over this man.

She responded by typing, I like your choice. Who doesn't love a man who'd slay a dragon for the woman he loves?

Three more dots appeared before disappearing. This happened a couple more times. Carly wondered what Jesse was writing. Or, rather, rewriting. She reread what she wrote and groaned. What if he took it as her wanting him to slay some fictional dragon for her? That wasn't what she had meant at all. She could slay her own dragons, thank you very much. Her fingers hovered on the keys, trying to think of what to say to cover her mistake. He responded before she could think of anything.

What are you doing Friday evening?

Carly bit her lip. What had Amy told her earlier? Something about not setting expectations too high when his headspace might not be in the same place as hers?

But that was before he sent her a picture of one of the greatest love stories in Greek mythology.

Nothing important.

Can I take you out again?

Carly didn't hesitate this time: Absolutely.

Chapter Twelve

When Carly chose her outfit for her date Friday night, she made sure she was dressed to the nines. Jesse had texted her that he was taking her somewhere nice, so she wore one of the rare dresses she had for nice dinners with sponsors. It was a black pencil dress with ruffled capped sleeves, a ruched middle, and more ruffles that ran along the left side, down to her knees. She had put her hair into a twist and wore dangling black beaded earrings to complete the look.

She eyed her reflection in the mirror critically, looking for any imperfections. She looked a little tense, but other than that, she couldn't see anything that could turn a man off.

If Jesse Abernathy didn't kiss her tonight, then she had the answer she'd been asking herself from the moment she met him.

He just wasn't that into her.

Maybe he asked her out for companionship. Or perhaps he was looking for friends, him being new to town like her. If that was what he wanted, then that was what she would give him. Even if it broke her heart. Especially if he started dating someone he actually *was* interested in and he came to her—his friend—to tell her all about the woman he *did* care about.

As usual, Jesse took her breath away when he greeted her at her door. Tonight he wore a black button-down shirt with matching black slacks. For once, he'd left his cowboy hat at home, leaving her fingers aching to run through the locks of his thick hair.

They were soon on their way. Carly fiddled with her purse in her lap, running her finger over the cool metal clasp.

"Everything okay?" Jesse asked as he drove the truck toward town.

"Yes," she replied, forcing herself to relax. Carly took a deep breath, enjoying the scent of fresh soap and Jesse's cologne. He smelled amazing, like amber and patchouli.

"How are things going at your place?" he asked. "Are you scratching at the walls to get back on the road?"

"Definitely not," Carly said. Out of the corner of her eye, she saw his hands loosen slightly on the steering wheel at her proclamation. Maybe she wasn't the only one nervous about tonight. "In fact, I started making inquiries to get my riding school up and running."

Jesse seemed content to let her prattle on about some horse rescues in the state that she'd been in contact with.

"Sounds like you're making progress," he said as they pulled into the parking lot of a historic-looking building. There was a blinking sign that was mounted on the brick wall above a set of stairs leading to the building's basement level.

"The Tenacity Social Club," she read. "What is this place?"

He grinned at her. "It's usually casual dining, but

they're doing a fundraiser tonight. The owner is doing a special menu for the night and brought in a jazz band."

Once they were out of his truck, he offered her his arm. "Shall we?"

They made their way down the steps. Carly could hear jazz music filtering through the stairwell. They entered the club, which had been decorated to look like a speakeasy from the 1920s with dark walls and forest-green chairs with tables made of mahogany. Candles flickered on tables, giving the atmosphere a romantic ambience. The place smelled like bourbon and wood polish.

A bar was situated in one corner and a stage was in the other, where a live band was performing. Couples swayed together on the herringbone dance floor. A couple of men sat at the bar, drinking their sorrows away, while a few couples sat the various tables eating food that smelled incredible. It was cozy yet cool at the same time. A few people noticed them and waved, making Carly smile in response. She was really starting to love small-town living.

A handsome man came over to them. He had on a midnight-blue shirt that bore the nametag *Mike*. "Welcome! We're doing a special event tonight. Do you have a reservation?"

"Yes, for Jesse, party of two," Jesse replied.

Mike led them to a table near the dance floor and handed them their menus. "Can I interest you in a wine? We have a Dino-themed red wine for the event."

"That sounds great to me," Carly said.

"I'll take that too," Jesse added.

Mike returned shortly with two glasses of wine. They gave him their food order—Jesse ordered a steak, while

Carly ordered a mushroom Wellington—and Mike hurried off to the kitchen.

"I feel like I talked my head off in the car," Carly said after taking a sip of the wine. It was just as amazing as Mike had said. She smiled softly at Jesse. "How was your week?"

Some of the relaxation that had been on Jesse's face while he listened to the band, dimmed slightly. "Oh, it was fine."

"Just fine?"

The side of Jesse's mouth ticked. "Oscar had a bit of a rough week at school. He thought some boys wanted to have lunch with him, but when he showed up at the table, it was already full. I think I mentioned he struggles to understand social cues sometimes. Instead of walking away like nothing happened, he started stimming at the table—"

"Stimming? Like the day I ran into you outside Town Hall?"

He smiled at her. "That was the light version. He does this thing where he clenches and unclenches his fists. He cut his palms with his nails this time, and they started to bleed, which made things worse. He then started flapping them around, and—let's just say kids can be really cruel, especially when faced with things they don't understand. People started laughing and pointing at him."

Carly reached across the table and placed her hand over his, giving it a quick comforting squeeze. "I'm so sorry, Jesse. What ended up happening?"

"A couple of the football players finally looked up from their lunches to notice Oscar. They were able to talk him into going to see Coach Finn, who then called me. By the time I got to the school, the damage was done. Oscar was red-eyed and sitting in the counselor's office, rocking himself. I didn't know what to say..."

He drifted off, and she was reminded of what he told her before—that he thought he was a failure of a parent compared to his wife.

"You were there for him," Carly said. "That's sometimes all a kid needs."

She thought back to her own struggles as a kid, and some of the nightmares of her childhood. There were nights when all she could do was pretend her birth parents were still with her, comforting her when her foster father started yelling or her foster brother began hitting her. It had been a coping mechanism to pretend her parents were still there, offering her comforting words in her ear. She'd get lost in her head, where her reality could never touch her.

"Thanks." Jesse lifted her hand and kissed it. Tenderness flooded her. He released her to take another sip of his wine. "Anyway, let's talk about something happier, huh?"

"Sure," she replied. "But... I'm here for you if you ever want to talk."

"I know." His smile was sweet as he looked at her. "I appreciate that."

"So...change of subject, then. How is it living with JenniLynn and Grayson and all the kids?"

Jesse laughed at that, and his body visibly loss its stiffness "Don't forget the dogs! It's lively, for sure."

They continued to talk until dinner arrived. Carly took a bite of her food, and her mouth instantly watered with pleasure. She savored the gravy on top, dipping her seasoned vegetables in it so she didn't miss a single bite.

After finishing their meal, she said, "It's incredible. I've been all over the world, but Tenacity has some of the best food I've ever eaten."

"I'm glad you approve," he said, his eyes soft. "Would you care to dance?"

"I'd love that."

They made their way onto the dance floor just as the band began to play a slow, melodic song. The trumpet player placed a mute on the bell of his instrument, giving it a timeless sound.

Carly wrapped her arms around Jesse's neck, her fingers playing with the hair at the base of his skull. It was just as soft as she thought it'd be. He put his own palms at the base of her spine, the heat of his hands seeping into the fabric of her dress. There was hardly any space between them, and she couldn't have asked for anything better. She almost wished that she had worn a looser skirt so that she could feel one of those strong thighs of his between her own. Her hand drifted to his chest, resting above his heart, taking comfort from the steady beat of it.

The music changed, the beat becoming faster. Carly thought perhaps that was the end of their dance. Instead, Jesse twirled her away from him, only to bring her back hard enough so that her breasts met his chest. He smirked at her surprised expression before he dipped her.

"What are you doing?" She laughed.

"Showing you that this guy has some moves." He wiggled his eyebrows at her.

She was very tempted to ask him to show her some more of those alleged moves when he brought her upright again, only to whirl her in his arms. They danced around the floor, cackling like loons. Other couples moved out of their way, and she was pretty sure she saw someone whip out their camera, but in that moment, she didn't care.

If she'd been keeping a tally of her best dates, this one would've taken a top spot without question.

When he drove her home later that night, she felt more optimistic about their relationship than she ever had before. She'd put off the question of whether he was really ready to date, but maybe now was the right time. Unlike the drive to their date, she didn't feel distracted or tense. She felt hopeful.

"I had a lot of fun tonight," he said as they stood on her porch, but he made no move to kiss her.

"I did too," she replied, leaning against the railing.

"Well, I…" he started to say before he gave her a tight smile. "I'll call you later, okay? Have a good night."

He started down the steps so he could head to his car. Carly shook her head as she watched him go. They had just spent an incredibly romantic evening together and he was walking away like nothing happened.

Carly's frustration boiled over and she followed him. "I need some clarity here."

He gave her a quizzical look. "Sure. What about?"

"Are we dating? Or do you want to be only friends?"

Jesse froze at that. "You don't know we're dating?"

"Are you really ready for this? I mean, it's okay if you're not—you must have really loved your wife—but just tell me if I don't have a chance here because—"

Jesse held up his hand to stop her tirade from spewing any further. "Forgive me, but I think I need to recap this conversation. You think that we're either not dating, I just want to be friends, or I'm not ready to date. Do I have that about right?"

Carly wanted nothing more than to run inside her house and never come out again. Ever. The police would eventually be called because the neighbors would complain about the smell wafting from the house, even though they lived miles away. And the real irony was that it'd be Jesse who made the call.

"It's getting pretty late," she said weakly. "I should get inside."

"Yeah, that's not going to happen."

Carly stiffened at that. "I'm sorry?"

"I need to understand what's going on in that head of yours."

She raised her chin. "I don't think that it's really that confusing."

"I might be just a dumb country boy, then, because I don't understand how we went from having an incredible night tonight to you asking me if I'm not interested in dating you."

Carly tried her best not to let hope rise in her at his words. Because he'd probably run for the hills after this conversation tonight.

"I thought maybe this wasn't working for you and you'd prefer for us to be friends. You don't call or text much and..."

Her voice trailed off as he ran a hand through his hair, making it stick up adorably. She refused to be distracted. His head dropped as he muttered, "I knew I was going to be bad at this. You only want to be friends?"

"No!" she was quick to answer. "I want us to date, but..."

His eyes locked on her. "But what?"

She looked up at the night sky, feeling humiliated. If

she still wished on stars, she would have begged to get out of this situation.

Jesse finally took a step toward her. "Talk to me."

"Why don't you want to kiss me?" When he looked at her with a completely stunned expression, her face flamed. She wanted nothing more than to go inside and cry. She muttered, "Forget it."

She turned to enter her house. She didn't make it two steps before Jesse grabbed her and swung her around to face him.

Before she could ask what he was doing, he cupped her cheeks and kissed her hard. She stiffened in shock for half a second before she relaxed into the kiss. Jesse loosened the pressure so he could angle his head. She gasped for air but was cut off as he kissed her again, his tongue dipping into her mouth. Hers danced with his in a sensuous rhythm. Jesse's hands drifted to the twist in her hair and began pulling out the bobby pins.

He pulled back enough to say, "I love your hair. I have dreams about it."

The locks tumbled wildly around her shoulders. Carly was sure it looked like she'd been electrocuted considering how much hairspray she'd put into it before she left the house, but she didn't care as she wrapped her arms around him and pulled his mouth back to hers with a moan.

His hands wrapped around her, his palms lowering until they were on her curvy bottom. He pulled her even closer, and she arched against him, desire pooling between her thighs.

He pulled away with a shuddering breath before leaning his forehead against hers. "I've wanted to kiss you from the first second I saw you. I definitely want to date you. I'm just a little out of practice… and I was trying to be a gentleman."

Carly licked at her lips, drawing his eyes in the faint light of her porch.

"Don't be a gentleman," she murmured.

With a groan, he pulled her back into his arms.

Chapter Thirteen

Carly drove down the road a few days later, humming to herself. Three nights ago, she and Jesse had made out on her front porch like a couple of teenagers, and then when their mouths were finally both too sore to kiss anymore, Jesse pulled back and said he needed to get going.

But before he left, he reached inside his pocket and pulled something out. He handed it to her with a wink and said *Good night, Carly* in a tone that made her shiver.

After he left and she went inside, she glanced down to see what he'd handed her. It had been the bobby pins he'd pulled from her hair. The sight of them made heat coil inside her all over again, and she'd gone in the bathroom to take a cool shower.

They'd spent the next day texting with silly little tidbits about what they were doing. Carly had to repair some stalls in her barn, while Jesse had to work on his future home. She'd sent him a picture of Nieve, and he'd responded that he could *feel* the horse's judgment through the pixels.

Carly was falling fast and hard, even as she tried to put a brake on her emotions. Just because Jesse was an incredible kisser and he'd confirmed he wanted to date, it didn't mean he wanted—or was ready to offer—forever with her. She needed to proceed with caution like she did with every other relationship in her life.

She was pulled from her thoughts when she saw a familiar teen walking down the road. What on earth was Oscar doing? He had his backpack on, and he was coming from the direction of the high school, but…he couldn't have walked the whole distance. The school was miles away.

She pulled up next to him and hit the button on the passenger side window. "Hey, Oscar," she called out as to not scare him. Lord knows she would not react well if a car pulled up next to her and she didn't know who the person was.

He stopped walking, but he didn't look at her. "Hi, Carly."

"Where you coming from?"

"School."

Carly's mouth dropped as he confirmed what she'd suspected. "That's pretty far away. Did you miss the bus?"

He sniffed. "Felt like walking."

He wiped at his eyes, and she could finally see that they were red and puffy.

Her heart cried for him. "You want to talk about what's wrong?"

Oscar didn't say anything. He kicked a pebble toward the side of the road.

"Come on," she encouraged. "I'll give you a ride home, and you can tell me all about it."

He hesitated for a second before his shoulders finally slumped and he dragged his feet over to the car. Once he was inside and buckled, she put the car in Drive again and they headed for the Abernathy property.

"So…" she said. "What's going on?"

His face was turned away as he stared out the window. "Did you hear that the football team is going to the district championship game next weekend?"

Remi and Shane had told her all about it. Given how far everything was from Tenacity, they planned on doing the drive to the stadium, which was an hour away.

"I did hear that," Carly said.

"It's an overnight trip. There's no way Dad will ever let me go." Carly noticed that Oscar's fists were closing and opening on repeat, a sign that he was starting to stim, from what Jesse had told her. "Coach Finn is really great and wants my advice, but the guys don't always want to listen. I'm tired of trying. I'm tired of this whole stupid town."

Carly was careful on how she answered. "Why do you want to go on this trip, then?"

The hands opened and closed even faster. "Because…"

When he didn't say anything, she pushed, "Yes?"

Oscar gave an exasperated sigh. "Because I love football, and if I go, then maybe they'll see that I have something to offer too. I'm not just the weird kid with all the stats who has to wear sensory headphones. Maybe they'll see *me*."

"Oh," Carly replied, finally understanding what was upsetting the teen. He had a chance to go off on an overnight trip with everyone else—to *be* like everyone else. This might be a great time for him to make some friends or for the kids to get to know him better at least.

"What did Coach Finn say?" she asked.

"He said he'd make sure I was treated fairly. The school put him in a suite, and he said I could have the spare room. So even though I'd be staying in the suite with the coaches, do you think Dad will let me go? No!"

They pulled up to the Abernathy property. "Let me talk to your dad," Carly finally said. "I can't promise you anything, but I'll see what I can do."

Oscar finally looked at her, and her insides lurched at the sad hopelessness on his face.

Once they pulled up to the house, Jesse stepped out onto the large porch. He seemed confused for a second before he saw who was in the car with her.

Jesse hurried over to them as they got out. "Oscar? What's wrong?"

Oscar didn't meet his eyes as he brushed by him. "Later, Dad." He stormed into the house, shutting the door firmly behind him.

Jesse rubbed at his face. "What the hell was that about?"

"I found him walking home from school—" Carly started to explain.

"What?" Jesse interrupted. "It's miles away. How could they let that happen? I'm going to call them right now."

He started to turn, but Carly grabbed his arm, stopping him. "Maybe give Oscar a chance to speak with you first before you chew out someone who doesn't deserve it."

Jesse was clearly frustrated, but he was careful with his response. "I appreciate your help, but Oscar shouldn't be walking this far."

"I understand that," Carly said. "He's also a teenage boy."

"I know, but as his father I need to be his advocate."

Carly knew she needed to back down. This was really

none of her business, but her emotions ached for Oscar. "He's a kid who wants to be a real part of the team."

Jesse looked away guiltily. "He told you, right? That the football team is going to their district game next weekend. They'll be spending the night in a hotel. Oscar wants to go."

"He told me," Carly confirmed. "You're worried."

The side of Jesse's mouth quirked up. "He's never spent the night with someone who wasn't family. I can't go because Grayson and I managed to screw up the HVAC install, and a professional is coming out to take a look at it, but they can only get to the ranch Saturday morning. I need to be on hand. Coach Finn assured me that he'd keep an eye on him, and he's been really good with Oscar so far, especially when he gets overstimulated, but what if it becomes too much? We're talking about a football stadium where the college a few towns over plays. That's a big crowd and a lot of screaming. What if it's too much for Oscar?"

"Have you talked to his school counselors? Teachers? Did any of them have any advice?"

"I talked to the counselor. He specializes in autism, and he seemed to think that Oscar would do all right as long as he wears his headphones."

"So…"

"It's still far away."

Carly looked at Jesse sadly. "I know you're worried, but I think Oscar really needs this. He loves you—I know he does—but do you ever think that maybe you're not giving him enough space to figure things out on his own and it's making him resentful?"

Jesse stiffened. "It's my job to protect him."

Carly's palms went to her hips. "I'm just saying he'll be in good hands if you let him go. The school has assured you of this. Let him live a little. Worst case scenario, my cousin Remi and Shane are going to the game. I can ask them to keep an eye on Oscar, and if things get bad, they can always bring him home."

A muscle ticked in Jesse's jaw before he said stiffly, "You think they'd do that for him?"

"I know they would," she responded.

Jesse nodded before glancing back at the closed door of the house. He lost some of his rigidness as he let out a deep sigh. "I'll think about it."

He took a step toward Carly and brushed his lips lightly against hers. "Thanks for driving Oscar home. I should go talk to him. I'll call you later."

"Okay." She squeezed his arm before he left.

Carly felt uneasy as she got back into her car. She hated the tension between father and son. But as much as she probably shouldn't have, she didn't regret speaking up on Oscar's behalf. For so long growing up, she'd felt helpless—like she didn't have any control over her own life. She hated that Oscar might even remotely feel like she had. He'd made it more than clear on multiple occasions that he resented his father's hovering.

Carly cared for Jesse. Deeply. And because of that, she worried that if he didn't loosen the reins a little on his son, he might end up losing the one person he loved the most.

Chapter Fourteen

A couple of days later, Jesse picked Oscar up from school. His son scowled when he saw him, but hopped into his truck.

"Are you making sure that I don't walk home again?" Oscar said, slouching in the seat.

Jesse counted to ten before he answered. "I thought we could work on the house this evening."

Oscar turned his head away to look out the window. "I'm surprised you trust me with a paintbrush."

Jesse put the truck in Drive. "Of course, I trust you."

"Then why won't you let me go on the trip this weekend?"

Jesse gritted his teeth. They had been having this argument for the past few days.

"I trust you," Jesse repeated. "But what if the crowd will be too much—"

"Carly said her cousin and her fiancée will be there, didn't she? If it gets to be too much, I'll ask them to bring me home. Or I'll let Coach Finn know."

Jesse really regretted Oscar overhearing him tell Grayson that Carly had offered her cousin's services. Oscar had been relentless about his request to go with the team ever since. The thing was no one saw how bad his son could get because he wasn't severely autistic. Jesse had and he worried that despite all the reassurances, they wouldn't be able to handle him. Oscar was already struggling with making friends in school. In a town as small as Tenacity, it'd break Jesse's heart if Oscar was ostracized.

"Let's focus on the house today, okay?" he practically pleaded.

Oscar didn't answer or say anything else for the rest of the drive. One of Oscar's favorite songs from his childhood came on the radio. He used to hum to it loudly from the back seat when he was a kid. Now there was nothing but the sound of the beat competing with the crunch of the dirt road under their tires.

Oscar wasn't a kid anymore. But that didn't stop him from stomping into the room that would eventually be his as soon as they reached the house. He probably would have slammed his door, but it wasn't installed yet.

Jesse ran a hand over his face before he went into the living room to get started. He grabbed the broom and began sweeping up the remaining construction debris. He wanted to get the house done. Everything felt so unsettled at the moment—like their lives were on pause until they could get their own roof over their heads.

Jesse put the broom away and got out the paint cans. He felt like he and Oscar were struggling so much lately. It was another reason Jesse was determined to get the house done. They were surviving off Jesse's job doing remote IT analytical work and the nest egg he'd saved over the years, but he was counting down the minutes until he could get back to ranching. He was restless for it. He wanted to get Oscar immersed into that life. It'd be good for him and give him an emotional outlet. It'd be good for Jesse too.

He needed to feel the open air again throughout his day instead of staring at numbers on a computer until his eyes crossed. If he could take the mental stress of getting the house done off his plate, then maybe he could work on fixing his fraying relationship with his son. He might also find a way to make things better between him and Carly so she'd never doubt him again.

The other day Grayson had brought up the idea of him and Jesse joining forces instead of having two separate ranches. Jesse liked the idea, especially as Grayson already had an established reputation in the industry. They'd have to discuss it more, but it was something to think about.

At the moment, he wasn't in the right frame of mind to make any huge decisions about the future. Aside from the tension between him and Oscar, he couldn't stop thinking about how he'd almost blown it with Carly.

As he looked over at the tiny kitchen, he couldn't help but think how much MaryBeth would have hated it. One of the reasons they'd bought the house in Houston was because of the large kitchen, which was MaryBeth's domain. Of course, she was perfectly happy living in the big city. She'd thrived on it, even if they were more in the suburbs.

I don't want to have to drive thirty miles just to get laundry detergent, she'd argued during one of their fights after Jesse brought up moving back to the country one day. She'd never wanted this kind of life. It was such a difference from Carly, who'd deliberately sought out the same lifestyle he had.

No, he wouldn't do that. He wouldn't compare the two. It was unfair to both of them.

As Jesse opened the can of paint and stirred it with the wood stick, he thought back to his last date with Carly. He couldn't believe he'd gotten everything so wrong. He thought it would be best to take things slow, to show her how committed he was. Instead, all he'd done was make her feel insecure about his intentions.

Though the end results of their conversation had been worth it. He could still feel the plumpness of her lip as he'd sucked it into his mouth. He could hear the moans she made, feel the way she arched against him.

Jesse dropped the stick into the can of paint and swore as it started to sink. He needed to stop thinking about those kisses before he embarrassed himself in front of his son. After rescuing the stick, he poured the paint into the awaiting pan. He grabbed a roller and started painting the wall, getting into a methodical rhythm as the drywall transformed into a creamy blue.

An hour later, he was starting to feel more relaxed as he worked off some tension, when he heard a crash in the other room. Jesse dropped the roller and ran to where Oscar was. Yellow paint had spilled all over the floor. Thankfully they hadn't installed the carpet yet.

Oscar was pacing back and forth in the paint, leaving footprints everywhere he stepped, his hands clenching and unclenching. "I'm sorry, I'm sorry, I'm sorry, I'm sorry, I'm sorry," he kept saying like a broken record.

"It's okay," Jesse replied, knowing that Oscar was stimming too much to calm down with mere words.

"I'm sorry, I'm sorry…" Oscar repeated.

"Bud, it's okay." Jesse didn't try to touch him. He

wouldn't unless Oscar started to hurt himself, which he used to do when he was younger. "Why don't we take a break and get some dinner."

"I'm sorry, I'm sorry…"

"Hey," Jesse said as calmly as he could. "I need some fresh air after all the paint fumes, and I brought your favorite sandwich—ham and mayo, just the way you like it."

Oscar's frantic pacing started to slow.

"I even bought a bag of JenniLynn's homemade cookies, but don't tell her I took a few."

"Cookies?" his son finally said. Jesse's heart shattered at the broken expression on his face.

"Yeah, the chocolate-chip ones, which I know are your favorite. Come on. Let's go eat."

He started to walk slowly out of the room and was relieved when Oscar followed him. He'd trek paint throughout the house, but that was fine. It was all wood boards anyway. They'd be covered up.

The duo walked outside and headed toward the truck. Jesse opened the back of the truck and reached inside for the cooler he'd packed earlier. Oscar sat down on the gate. Jesse put the food between them and sat on the other side.

They ate in silence for several minutes, before Jesse broached the subject. "Was that about this weekend?"

"I… I guess," Oscar replied, picking at a piece of bread.

"Talk to me," Jesse encouraged.

"I'm tired of not having any friends and feeling like a freak."

"You're not a freak," Jesse insisted.

"Aren't I?" Oscar looked at him with the saddest eyes he'd ever seen. "Because the rest of the team gets to go, and both the coach and Carly have told you that I'll be in safe hands, but I still can't be like other kids."

He looked so defeated. Jesse glanced away, toward the direction of Carly's homestead.

He loves you, she'd said. *I know he does—but do you ever think that maybe you're not giving him enough space to figure things out on his own?*

Carly and Oscar were right. Oscar would never get to live the life Jesse wanted for him if he didn't allow him to be more independent. Jesse could keep him locked away like damned Rapunzel, or he could let him leave the tower and taste what others got to experience. Because if Jesse didn't give him a little bit of freedom, he had a feeling it'd only stress Oscar even worse.

"Okay…" he finally said before he could change his mind. "You can go."

Oscar whipped his head to him. "What?"

"You can go," Jesse said more firmly. "But I want you to text me when you get there, and you promise that you'll tell Coach Finn if you start to feel even slightly off."

"I will," Oscar told him sincerely. He unexpectedly threw his arms around Jesse and hugged him. "Thanks, Dad."

Oscar hopped off the truck and hurried inside the house. Jesse stared after him with worry and love vying for control of his limbic system. Oscar rarely liked being touched by others, let alone giving out hugs willingly. Jesse couldn't remember the last time they *had* hugged. His heart melted.

Please let him be safe.

He scrunched up the wax paper he'd used to wrap up

his sandwich. He was feeling uneasy and needed someone else's assurance that he'd just done the right thing.

Jesse hopped off the tailgate and pulled his phone out of his pocket. He dialed Carly's number and waited for her to answer.

"C'mon, baby," he said before realizing the nickname that he'd given her. The call went to voicemail, and he hung up, shocked that *baby* had slipped out so easily.

He was getting in way over his head.

Jesse pulled up their text message chain and read the last one Carly sent him, stating that she'd planned on practicing with Nieve all week so she'd be prepared to perform for the Dinosaur Day Rodeo.

That was something else he worried a lot about. Jesse knew that the rodeo was a huge part of Carly's life, but he worried every time she brought it up. He'd done his best to hide his concern and support any decisions she made for herself. That didn't stop him from wanting to go all caveman on her and tell her he didn't want her returning to the circuit.

He would have too, if he didn't think Carly would bust a rib laughing. She was not the type of woman to let a man make a decision for her—it was honestly part of her charm. Besides, he'd already almost blown their relationship. He was surprised she hadn't already shown him to the door.

He couldn't help but worry though whenever she talked about rodeo life. There was a part of him that was scared she'd find the allure too much—especially once she was in front of the crowds again at the Dinosaur Days event—and she'd feel the urge to return to the road. But that was nothing compared to what worried him the most.

He was terrified something would happen to Carly and she'd die just like MaryBeth had. He hadn't forgotten what Oscar had told him when they'd met her that first time. Carly had been injured in the past year. And though she brushed it off when he'd tried to bring up his concern, he knew people died doing what she did for a living. It was just his luck, falling for someone who had a dangerous job. He'd go out of his mind if he found a new chance at happiness, only for that love to be taken away again. He doubted he'd be able to recover a second time.

"Dad," Oscar called out. "What are we going to do about the mess?"

And wasn't that the question of the century.

Chapter Fifteen

The next Saturday, Carly headed to Tenacity Grocery. Things were pretty quiet in town, even for a place as small as Tenacity. It was different than earlier in the week, when there was a buzz in the air leading up to the district football game. A lot of people had decided to tailgate over to the stadium, leaving most of Tenacity like a ghost town. That worked fine for Carly.

Whenever she made her way into town, she always had people coming up to her to ask her about the upcoming Fall Dinosaur Days since word got out that she planned on performing at the rodeo. If they weren't asking about that, they were asking about Jesse. She was happy to smile and take pictures when it came to anything regarding the rodeo.

But Jesse was a subject she wasn't as eager to talk about.

Things were fine since she'd advised him to give Oscar some space. Perfectly…fine.

They'd texted throughout the week, though not as much as they had been. She'd asked him if everything was okay at one point, and he'd said he was busy painting his house. That was fair, even if it felt like there was a growing distance between them. She hadn't asked him what he ended up deciding regarding Oscar going with the football team, but Jesse had texted her earlier that morning asking if he could come over and talk.

She'd stared at her phone for a whole five minutes before she finally responded that she'd get some snacks. He'd responded that he'd bring a pizza. Pizza had to be a good sign, right? She didn't know what kind of talk Jesse wanted to have, but what kind of sadist dumped someone over pizza?

Carly pulled into an available spot outside of Tenacity Grocery and put her car in Park. She walked out and headed toward the brick two-story building. Two elderly men sat outside, shooting the breeze with one another. They stopped talking as she approached.

"Howdy, Ms. Hawkins," the one man said. He had salt-and-pepper hair that was mostly gone and wore a flannel shirt. He looked at her over the rim of his glasses. "What brings you to town this beautiful fall afternoon?"

His companion elbowed him, and the man guffawed.

"What do you think she's doing at a grocery store, you ninny?" the other man said. This one was tall and gangly with a gray mustache.

"I'm just making conversation."

"You're being nosy. You just want the scoop on what's happening between her and Jesse Abernathy." The taller man looked at her. "Forgive Gary—he's been married to my sister for too long. They're both busybodies."

Gary glared at his brother-in-law. "I'm going to make sure to tell her you said that, Richard."

Richard gulped. "You wouldn't dare."

Carly shook her head and left the men to their squabbling as she entered the store. A bored teenager behind the counter waved to her, and she smiled back.

She grabbed a basket and walked around the store getting some microwave popcorn, licorice, and a case of hard seltzer. If Jesse planned on breaking up with her, she was going to binge-watch TV while stuffing her face with as many empty calories as she could.

"Hello!" a woman called from behind the meat counter, her voice bright over the low hum of the coolers. "Are you excited for the upcoming rodeo?"

"Very," Carly replied, offering a polite smile as she adjusted the grocery basket on her arm.

There was a good chance this rodeo might be her last, and she wanted to enjoy it. She owed herself that much. Still, the thought carried more weight than she wanted to admit. Rodeo had been her world for so long. But lately, when she thought about her career—the endless travel, the pressure to stay at the top, the constant spotlight—retirement sounded more appealing than ever.

She was tired. Not just the kind of tired that a good night's sleep could fix, but the deep, bone-level exhaustion that came from years of being on. Always performing. Always smiling. Always needing to be the best. Somewhere along the way, the joy had started to slip through her fingers. Especially after the disaster with Fletch.

"My whole family's planning on attending," the worker continued as she wrapped a package of steaks in brown paper for a different customer. "It's not every day we get to see a celebrity perform."

Carly's lips curved politely. "Thank you for attending."

The woman beamed. "We're all huge fans in my household. My daughter was just heartbroken when you and

Fletch Alistair broke up. She's been following your career for years! She honestly thought you two would get married—"

Carly's fingers tightened around the basket handle. A dull ache stirred in her chest, but she kept her tone steady. "No, neither of us planned on that. I—"

"That's what I said," the woman cut in with a cheerful shrug. "Besides, Jesse Abernathy is much cuter, in my opinion. And he's local." She gave Carly a knowing wink.

Carly blinked, caught off guard. "Oh—well…it was nice talking to you." She shifted her basket higher on her arm. "I should get going."

She turned down the nearest aisle before the woman could respond, her pulse quickening. The overhead lights hummed softly, and for a moment she just stood there between the shelves of coffee and cereal, trying to breathe. She hadn't realized her life in Australia had made such an impact here—that strangers, halfway across the world, still followed gossip about her and Fletch.

And just like that, the walls she'd built between her old life and this new one felt a little thinner.

Once she was done with her purchases, she headed back outside. Gary and Richard were gone, and she wondered if they'd gone to rat each other out to Gary's wife. It was almost too bad. She could have used the distraction.

After she got home, she quickly tidied up the house. Carly wasn't inside much anyway, considering she spent a majority of her time outside working on her potential school and practicing for the upcoming rodeo. Time was also ticking away on her getting back to Dex, but she'd worry about that tomorrow. If Jesse told her tonight that he was done with her meddling, then maybe she would take her agent up on his offer. At least for a little while. It wouldn't be running away by any means. Just…a return to her roots.

She went into her room to get ready, deciding on yoga pants and a pullover sweatshirt that hung loosely over one shoulder. She figured she might as well be comfortable tonight, especially depending on how things turned out. She thought about ditching her bra, but her breasts were big enough that it'd be too noticeable. Then again, this might end up being a really short conversation, so to hell with it. She was just pulling her hair into a loose ponytail when there was a knock on the door. She ran to answer it, wanting to get the evening over with.

"Hey," Jesse said, holding a box from Pete's Pizza and a six-pack of beer.

"Hi," she said before stepping back so he could come in. Carly headed to the kitchen and knew that Jesse was following. He set the pizza on the black dining table while she grabbed some plates from the cupboard.

When she turned around and saw Jesse taking in her casual clothes, his gaze lingering on the lack of bra strap that her loose sweatshirt revealed, her eyebrow raised. He tore his eyes away and flipped open the pizza box. On one half was pepperoni and mushroom; on the other was pineapple and black olives. She grabbed a seltzer out of the fridge and walked back to the table. Carly sat in one of the orange chairs at the table and pulled one of the slices toward her that was slathered in pineapple. She took a bite, taking a second to appreciate the salt and sweet deliciousness.

"I don't think I've known someone who likes pineapple on pizza before," Jesse said as he reached for a pepperoni slice.

"Have you ever tried it?" she countered.

He looked disgusted. "Absolutely not."

"Maybe I'll convert you yet," she said before licking away the sauce that was lingering on her lips.

He stilled before saying quietly, "Maybe you will."

She looked up at him and saw that he was staring at her mouth. Carly cleared her throat, wanting—needing—to get any impending heavy conversation over with. She cracked open the can of hard seltzer and took a swig before she said, "What did you want to talk about?"

She held her breath waiting for him to say that despite the looks he was giving her tonight, he wanted to end things. That she'd stuck her nose into his business one too many times. He was done with her. The story of her life.

Jesse grabbed a beer and twisted the cap off, taking his own drink before answering. "I wanted to say you were right."

Her forehead scrunched. "What?"

"You were right. About Oscar. I worry about him. All the time. I'm doing everything that I can to help him succeed, but I know I'm holding on too tight sometimes. I can't seem to stop worrying though."

"About what?" Carly asked, her tone gentle.

"That something will happen that he won't bounce back from. The idea of anything happening to him makes me crazy."

Carly fiddled with the tab on her can. "You can't keep him in a bubble forever."

"I know. You helped me realize that." Jesse took another swallow of his beer. "That's why I said he could go to the game."

Carly's eyes shot to his. "You did?"

"I did. He's currently at a hotel with his team as we speak."

"What'd he say when you said yes? How'd he react?"

The side of Jesse's mouth tilted up. "I haven't seen him that happy in I don't know how long. It was the right call to make. And I wanted to make sure you knew that I'm aware I was wrong. And that I appreciate what you said."

Carly took a couple of breaths in and out before she buried her face in her hands.

Jesse jumped up from where he was sitting opposite her and hurried around the table. "What is it?"

She shook her head, unable to speak.

"Baby, tell me what's wrong."

Her pulse sped up at the endearment.

"I thought you were going to break up with me," she muttered, her voice muffled against her hands.

"What? I can't—" He pulled her hands away, eyeing her in concern. "I can't understand what you're saying when your mouth is covered."

She didn't look at him. Instead she stared at his shoulder. "I thought you were coming over to break up with me."

"I don't want to break up." He kneeled on the floor next to her. "Why on earth would you think that?"

She finally met his eyes. "You said we needed to talk."

A line formed between Jesse's eyebrows. "No… I said I wanted to talk to you. When people say, 'We need to talk,' that usually suggests a relationship is over, which is not what I said. Why do you think I'm always on the verge of ending things with you?"

"Stifling abandonment issues?" she grumbled under her breath. "I don't know. Forget I said anything."

Jesse sat back on his heels. "I don't want you to keep thinking I'm going to break up with you. I'm the one out of my league here, not you."

He said it lightly, and she snorted in response despite the heavy conversation.

He reached up and tucked a loose strand of hair that had slipped from her ponytail. "You… My life has gotten so much better since you entered it. You call me out on my crap, and you make me laugh. You've helped me reach my son when I didn't think I could anymore. I love texting with you—even though I'm the first to admit that I'm crap at it. But you have no idea how much I look forward to starting my day just because I know there's a morning text from you. And I feel like the luckiest person in the world when I get a message from you wishing me a good night. You've filled an emptiness in my soul that I never thought I'd be able to fill again, so please stop thinking I'm going to break up with you."

Carly sniffled. "I feel the same way about you," she whispered.

"Okay," he responded. He stood up and offered her his hand. When she took it, he said, "Now, lead me to the couch so I can cuddle the hell out of you."

She burst out laughing as they made their way into her living room, sitting on her oversized white couch. She grabbed her controller and turned the TV on.

"Feel like watching anything in particular?" she asked.

"Anything but true crime or hospital dramas," he said.

When she gave him a questioning look, he said, "There's already enough unhappiness in the world. I don't need to hear any more about how depraved society is. And hospital dramas bring back bad memories."

"Got it," she said. She flipped the channels until they landed on a rom-com. "Good with this?"

"Fine with me," Jesse replied. He threw his arm around her and drew her close. She wrapped an arm around his waist, side hugging him. They settled in and started to watch the movie. She occasionally felt him brush his lips against her hair.

As the movie went on, Carly began to run her fingers up and down the smoothness of Jesse's flannel shirt. She soon became distracted as different parts of his abs twitched at her touch so she continued to tease the muscles.

"Carly, I'm trying to take things slow and be a gentleman here, but if you keep touching me like that, I'm going to return the favor."

Carly leaned slightly back so she could see Jesse's face. "Who says I want you to be a gentleman?"

He groaned before he clasped the back of her neck and pulled her mouth to his. Her hands ran up his sides, her palms pressing against his pecs. As their kiss deepened, their tongues played with each other.

His hand ran down her back, along her hips before settling on her bottom, molding her roundness. Before she knew it, Jesse pulled her into his lap so that she was straddling him. His hands shifted up, running along her ribs until they cupped her breasts, his thumbs running circles around her nipples through her sweatshirt.

She wanted to feel more of him—all of him. Carly leaned back and ripped the sweatshirt off her head.

Jesse stared at her revealed skin, muttering, "I'd wondered..." before he cupped a breast and leaned down to lick her hard nipple. Carly arched as he savored her, her hands tightening in his hair. She ground down on his lap, feeling how much he wanted her. Her body responded in return, going liquid with anticipation.

Jesse pulled back, his pupils blown wide open. "Do you—" His next breath looked like it pained him. "Do you want to stop?"

An onslaught of tenderness for this man only made her need him more.

"Don't you dare think about stopping," she replied, rubbing down on his lap once more.

He hissed before he pushed her to the side so he could stand up on unsteady legs. "Your couch is very comfortable, but I'm going to need more room to give you everything I've been planning in my head since the moment I laid eyes on you."

Carly shivered at that. "You promise?"

He pulled her against him and then picked her up, allowing her to wrap her legs around his waist as he carried her in the direction she pointed toward her bedroom.

"I guarantee it."

Chapter Sixteen

As Jesse pulled away from her much later, Carly did her best to control her rapid breath. She stared at the ceiling, trying to get her reeling emotions under control. She'd give him this—he definitely kept his guarantee.

She stretched, her body aching delectably in all the right spots. "Wow, if that's what you're like when you're trying to be a gentleman, I can't wait to see what you're like when you're not."

He didn't say anything, and her head angled toward him. His chest was rising as fast as hers was. The moonlight shone through the windows, highlighting his face. It was more serious than she'd ever seen it. Carly bit her lip.

"Are you, um, are you okay over there?" she asked, tentative. After their open communication earlier, she'd expected something—jokes, tender confessions of love—anything but the uncomfortable silence that was building between them.

"Yeah..." He pushed back the sheets and sat up. "Can I use your bathroom?"

"Sure," she said, pointing to the closed door across the room. Jesse got out of bed, his firm naked backside on full display. She couldn't appreciate it like she wanted to, not with her stomach twisting in knots. Was he regretting what they'd done? A chill that had nothing to do with the fall night had her shivering. She reached down and pulled the sheets back up so that they covered her exposed breasts.

She turned on her side so she faced the bedroom door, away from where he disappeared. She counted the minutes on the clock, waiting for him to return. The sound of the faucet turning on and water running filled the tense silence of the room. It took ten minutes before the door finally cracked open again with a quiet squeak. She immediately shut her eyes and took even breaths so that he would think that she had fallen asleep.

After experiencing such pure magic with this man, the night had suddenly soured, and she wanted nothing more than to cry.

"Carly?" he whispered her name. She didn't answer. He could wait until the morning to tell her it was a mistake.

She half expected him to gather his clothes and sneak out of her room. Instead, she felt the sheets lift off of her slightly and the mattress dip as he climbed into bed next to her. The heat of him soon warmed the sheets, taking away some of the chill she'd experienced at his abrupt departure. She felt him turn and wondered if he was facing her way or had his back to her. Was he staring at her, his face full of regret? She didn't look.

Her own tormented question was soon answered when she felt the light brush of his fingers tracing down her spine. He let out a quiet sigh and turned again. When she heard his breath even out, she buried her head in her pillow. A couple of tears seeped out, and she wiped them away with the edge of her pillowcase. Thankfully, her lids grew heavier and she eventually fell asleep.

* * *

When Carly woke the next morning, Jesse was gone. She reached across the mattress where he'd slept. The sheets were cool. The only sign that he'd slept next to her was the slight indent on the pillow. She tried not to let the fact that he'd left without telling her goodbye get to her, or her doubts plague her like they always did.

She was Carly-freaking-Hawkins. Her happiness did not depend on how a man treated her.

Then why did she feel so terrible?

Because…being abandoned triggered trauma from her youth that she just couldn't seem to let go, no matter how successful she'd become. There could very well be a good reason that Jesse left her at the crack of dawn. Maybe he'd received a message that Oscar hadn't done as well as they'd all hoped, and he'd had to run out to help his son. Perhaps Grayson needed him for something. There could be a million and one reasons that Jesse had to leave this morning, other than the worst-case scenario.

She grabbed fresh clothes and went into the bathroom. As she stood under the warm water, she tried to focus on what she needed to do for the day. But her mind kept going back to the night before. Jesse had told her that he didn't want to end things with her. She knew he meant it, and she felt confident that they were on the same page there.

What she hadn't realized until last night was that their problem wasn't her paranoia that Jesse would abandon her like half the people in her life had. No…their problem was that Jesse might not have any room for her inside his broken heart, and maybe he'd realized that after sleeping with her. And if that was the case, would he ever?

As she wiped the steam from the mirror, she stared at her blurry reflection. What had MaryBeth looked like? Been like? She had to be amazing considering what a good kid Oscar was, though Jesse deserved a lot of credit for that as well. Carly knew he'd never accept it.

But…what if Jesse had pretended that she was his beloved wife last night, and when he woke up this morning and saw her instead, he was given a reality shock?

She winced at that. No. No matter how many despairing thoughts she had about last night and herself at the moment, she couldn't and wouldn't believe that he was that crass.

"You need to pull yourself together," she muttered to her reflection. "You've been through a lot of worse things than a broken heart. And you don't even know if you have a reason to feel this way yet."

Once she got her bearings and insecurities under control, she'd follow up with Jesse and figure out exactly what had happened the previous night.

She got dressed and was in the middle of pulling her still-damp hair into a bun when she heard a knock on the door. She half hoped it was Jesse. It wasn't.

A familiar woman stood on her porch. Behind her in the driveway was a delivery truck with flowers painted on the side. Underneath the flowers were the words *Tiffany in Bloom*.

"Tiffany, hello!" Carly said, forcing a smile to her lips. She had only met Tiffany Brandt a couple of times through her cousin Remi. Tiffany was engaged to Ellis Corey, brother to Remi's fiancé, Shane. The two brothers were close, which was why the four had decided to have a joint wedding.

"Hi, Carly," Tiffany responded. "The house is looking good."

"Thanks," she replied. "Most of it came move-in ready, thank goodness, but I'm still working on the rest of the property. How are you doing? Getting excited for the wedding?"

"More so excited to marry Ellis." She laughed. "The florist for the wedding is being a bridezilla wanting perfection."

Despite her mood, Carly smiled at that, knowing full well that Tiffany was doing the flowers.

"Honestly," Tiffany continued, "I think I might be driving Remi insane. I found her pacing the other day, muttering something about yellow daffodils."

Carly did laugh at that, remembering the day she'd taken Remi with her to get Jesse a pie. Her cousin had been frayed then as well.

"Maybe you should take over flower duty completely," Carly suggested. "To be honest, I don't think Remi knows that much about which flowers look good with what."

Tiffany nodded, though she looked concerned. "I just want everything to be perfect. I don't want Remi to think I ruined her wedding because I picked the wrong color."

"She won't," Carly assured her. "Maybe you two can decide on another task she can take over on while you deal with the flowers."

Tiffany brightened. "We do still need to pick out our dinner settings for the reception."

"There you go, then. That sounds right up Remi's alley." She smiled before tilting her head. "Well, as pleased as I am to see you, what brings you to this neck of the woods?"

"Oh!" Tiffany said, remembering why she was there. She reached into the crate she was carrying and pulled out a vase of gorgeous pink roses. "Special delivery for you."

"Wow," Carly murmured, taking in the perfection of the dewy petals. "These are beautiful."

Tiffany wiggled her eyebrows. "Someone must really like you, huh?"

Carly pulled the flowers close to her chest and breathed them in, taking a moment to appreciate their scent. "Thank you so much."

She didn't comment on Tiffany's hint for information. The florist had to already know who the flowers were from.

They said their goodbyes, and Carly went back into the kitchen. She noticed that the pizza box from the night before was on top of her garbage container and that their empty bottle and can were in her sink. A little lump formed in Carly's throat realizing that Jesse must have cleaned up a little while she was sleeping.

She put the flowers on the table, running a finger over the silken petals. She searched for a card and noticed one buried between the green leaves. Pulling it off its plastic stem, Carly read the message.

I didn't want to wake you, but I had to pick up Oscar. Thank you for the amazing night. I'll call you later today. Jesse.

Then he'd drawn three hearts after his name. Carly's mouth broke into a smile as she traced one with the tip of her fingernail. She felt silly for letting her imagination run away with her earlier, when a part of her brain had been loudly shouting that there was a reasonable explanation as to why he'd left so early. She ran her thumb over the tiny heart Jesse had drawn next to his name. She knew she'd probably analyze what it meant for the rest of the day.

Her earlier confusion and hurt at his abrupt departure that morning ebbed slightly, though she couldn't help but feel a little out of sorts at how he'd acted right after they'd shared such a pleasurable moment together.

Carly needed to clear her head, so she grabbed her coat and headed for the barn to feed Nieve and clean his stall. Once they were through, she led him out into the rebuilt paddock so that he could graze and get his morning exercise.

As she stood along the fence, watching him, he sauntered over to her and gently nudged her arm.

"Hello, my handsome boy," she murmured against his soft forehead. "We should go for a ride later—what do you think?"

He whinnied in response before he trotted back over to a patch of grass. Carly left him to it. As she walked back to the barn, she breathed in the fresh cool air. The leaves were starting to change, leaving the homestead looking like nature had painted it in bright shades of red, yellow, and orange. No matter how conflicted she'd felt over the decisions she'd made in recent months, she would never regret buying this property.

She looked at the large patch of cement next to the barn. She assumed that the previous owners had used the space for horse trailers or equipment at some point. She stood on it and looked down at the hard surface beneath her feet.

She thought back to what her father had said all those weeks ago. Wouldn't this be the ideal spot for her office?

It'd be close to the barn and the perfect place to greet students if she opened her program.

Carly could almost picture the kids being bussed in from whatever foster system they were currently in. She wondered if, as she had that first time, they'd look at the horses with excitement, a little fear, and the feeling that her life would never be the same again because she'd been given a taste of freedom. That no matter what happened next for her, she'd always have that memory, and no one could ever take it away from her.

She wanted to do that for someone who was as lost as she'd once been. Could she do it though? Would she succeed at giving a child that feeling she'd had the first time her dad put her on a horse?

She wouldn't know unless she tried. But that meant… she had to let go of another part of her life.

A lick of excitement danced through her as she thought back to her vision of what she wanted to do with the property. She had the permits ready to go, contacts had been made to the different horse rescues. Amy's husband had put her in contact with some local contractors that he knew. If she did want to move forward with things, she had referrals she could call.

What was she waiting for? Doing the rodeo circuit was her job, something she did to give her financial security. The school was her dream. She had the means to do it. She just needed the gumption.

Taking a deep breath, she sent the contractor a text. And then…she called Dex.

Chapter Seventeen

Oscar was beaming by the time Jesse reached the school, where the buses had dropped off the team.

"Hey, bud," Jesse said, taking in his son's bright grin. "How'd it go?"

"It went great," Coach Finn said as he came up to them. The former professional football player gave Oscar a proud nod. "Oscar had all the stats on the opposing team. He suggested a play. I agreed and so did the team captain. It helped us win the game. The whole team now realizes what an asset he is."

"That he is," Jesse replied. Oscar studied sports like an art student studied Van Gogh.

"They made me team statistician," Oscar announced, rocking on his feet.

"The team was in agreement," Finn added.

Jesse's chest tightened proudly. He could read between the lines. The team had finally accepted his son.

His heart was in his throat as he smiled at Oscar. "It sounds like the trip was successful."

Finn nodded, his expression turning determined. "Yep. Especially now that the team knows we have a secret weapon in our midst."

He winked at Oscar, who stood a little straighter. Jesse

tried very hard to fight back the large grin that wanted to appear on his face. He didn't want to make things awkward for his son by pumping a victory fist in the air. He couldn't wait to tell Carly.

The thought of her brought him back to the night before. Their connection had been like a match to a stick of dynamite. Incredible. Explosive. Jesse ached to be near her again, whether to have sex or just to be beside her, he didn't care as long as he was with her.

Because he was in love with her.

He had a feeling he knew that leading up to what happened between them last night. Aside from Oscar, Carly was quickly becoming the most important person in his life. After they'd made love, he'd gone into the bathroom, feeling unsteady from the way she'd completely undone him. He'd had to stay there for countless minutes as his heart pounded with the reckoning of his feelings for her. He knew it was too soon in their relationship to be blurting out declarations of love, but he needed her in a way he hadn't felt in years.

And that was the thing. She made him *feel* again. He felt like he'd finally woken up from a ten-year coma. She made him laugh and worried the hell out of him. She called him out on his mistakes and made him feel like he was home whenever he was with her. He hated leaving her that morning.

He wished they could have talked before he'd left, but after he'd come out of the bathroom, she'd been asleep, and he hadn't wanted to rouse her. He should have gone home—she hadn't asked him to stay the night—but he couldn't fathom the idea of leaving her after what they'd shared. So instead, he'd gotten back in bed with her, moving as carefully as possible so he didn't wake her. Despite not wanting to disturb her, he hadn't been able to resist touching the soft skin of her back, tracing the delicate bones of her spine. She was it for him. Now he needed to be patient so that he could eventually convince her of that.

As he and Oscar walked to the truck, he asked, "Are you hungry?"

"We ate at the hotel, but that was forever ago, so yeah."

Jesse snorted. "Forever" was actually about a couple of hours ago, but Oscar was a teenager. He was always hungry.

"Why don't you and I get some brunch at the Silver Spur Café," Jesse suggested. "And then you can tell me all about yesterday."

"Okay," Oscar replied.

Together, father and son made their way to the center of town, the world a little brighter for both of them. Thanks to Carly.

Carly walked toward the center of town, pulling her fall coat a little tighter to her. She was supposed to meet the contractor soon to go over some of the ideas she had for the school.

"Carly!" someone called out, and she looked around to see who it was.

JenniLynn Garrett came over to her, a warm smile on her face.

"Hello, Mayor," Carly replied.

The other woman waved that off. "Please call me JenniLynn. I mean, you're dating my boyfriend's brother, right?"

Carly's lips compressed. "Right."

JenniLynn eyed her reaction, her smile turning to concern. "Uh-oh, what did he do?"

"Nothing. Everything is fine."

The mayor made a tsking noise. She grabbed Carly's arm and led her over to one of the benches in front of Tenacity Grocery.

As they both settled, JenniLynn said, "Okay, spill."

"I don't have anything to spill," Carly insisted. Her feelings were confusing enough as it was. She couldn't very well blabber how hurt she'd been by Jesse's reaction after they made love.

JenniLynn shook her head. "You know I'm also in love with an Abernathy man. I love Grayson dearly, but when people google the 'strong and silent type,' I guarantee you'd see a picture of the Abernathy men. They have huge hearts, but they aren't the best at expressing themselves."

"I..." Tears filled Carly's eyes, and before she knew it, she was telling JenniLynn everything. As she finished, she said, "I don't know...maybe there was only room in his heart for one woman, and she passed away."

JenniLynn stared across the road, her face reflective. "I never met MaryBeth, so I can't speak on Jesse's relationship with her. I know that he loved her. I think that's fair considering she was the mother of his child."

"I didn't mean—"

"I know you didn't mean anything by it," she assured her. "From what Grayson told me, Jesse lost his way for a long time after she died. It wasn't expected. She passed from a brain aneurysm."

Carly sucked in a shocked breath. "I didn't know that. Jesse never told me what happened other than she died."

JenniLynn nodded at that. "I can understand why. From

what Grayson told me, Jesse came home from work one day, found Oscar screaming his head off and MaryBeth unconscious on the floor. She died shortly after they got her to the hospital. There was nothing they could do. Jesse distanced himself from everyone except Oscar. He protects Oscar like his life depends on it. Part of it, I think, is because of Oscar's autism. I get that. My youngest is also on the spectrum, and it's impossible to not worry about them and what their future might be like. I think another part of it is his fear of losing another person he loves. But ever since he met you, I've noticed a change in him. He smiles more. He gives Oscar more space to grow and become his own man. It's a good thing—you being in his life." She reached over and squeezed Carly's arm. "Be patient with him. Because I can tell you from firsthand knowledge, these Abernathy men are worth it."

Carly nodded. They said their goodbyes, and Carly headed over to the Silver Spur Café, where a tall, handsome man stood outside, texting someone on his phone. His sleeves were rolled up, showcasing tattoos on both arms. He was the type of man who stopped women in their tracks. It was too bad Carly's heart was already consumed by Jesse.

"Hi," she said as she came up to him. "I don't suppose you're Connor Adair?"

"That I am," he replied, flashing a professional smile. "You must be Carly."

"Yes, it's nice to meet you."

"You too." Connor nodded toward the café. "Let's grab some coffee while you tell me about your plans. I work better with a cup of caffeine in front of me."

"Same." She laughed. "Lead the way."

They entered the café and were shown to the seating area to the right. After they slid into the booth, a middle-aged woman came up to them, introduced herself as Francine, and took their coffee orders.

"So," Connor started, "Josh said you're looking to build a riding school for foster kids."

"I am," Carly said. "I spent my early childhood in foster care. It wasn't until my parents took me in and put me on a horse for the first time that I felt safe. I want kids in similar situations to have the same experience."

"And you're going to bring in horses bound for the slaughterhouse?" he asked, and when she nodded, he smiled. "That sounds like an incredible project that I'd love to help out with. Have you looked into running it as a nonprofit? It can give me more options in terms of cutting pricing."

"Oh…" Carly responded. "I hadn't thought about that."

"You should," Connor encouraged. "I work pretty closely with some agencies throughout the area who can help you get it established. I can send you some names later if you want."

"That'd be amazing," Carly said, thankful for the help. She'd planned on using her name to connect with sponsors who were known for funding these types of projects. Telling them that they could possibly get a nice tax break could be just the incentive she needed to get them to commit.

Connor nodded before he said, "Give me an idea of what you're looking for."

"Well…" She pulled her phone out of her purse. "This is the current barn where I plan to stable the horses. It has a cement slab to the left of the main door, and I thought that might be the ideal spot for an office. You see right—"

"Carly?"

Carly dropped her phone as her head whipped to see Jesse standing beside her table. Oscar was with him.

"H-hi," she sputtered. Jesse looked from her to Connor then back to her, so she said, "This is Connor Adair. Connor, this is Jesse Abernathy and his son, Oscar."

"Nice to meet you," Connor said, continuing to keep things professional.

Jesse nodded, but his eyes didn't stray from Carly.

"Carly, guess what!" Oscar said. "Coach Finn promoted me to team statistician."

"That's amazing!" she replied, smiling brightly at the teen.

"Oscar, didn't you say you needed to use the restroom before we leave?" Jesse asked.

Oscar rolled his eyes, but he waved to the occupants in the booth before heading to the bathrooms in the back.

Jesse turned his full attention back to Carly. "Can I talk to you for a second?"

Carly glanced at Connor. They were in the middle of a business meeting. She didn't want to be rude.

Connor scooted out of the booth, solving the issue for her. "I needed to follow up with my assistant on something anyway. I'll be back, and we can continue our discussion."

She gave him an apologetic look but was grateful. "Sounds good."

As soon as he left, Jesse slid into his spot.

"Is there any reason you're interrupting my business meeting?" Carly asked him.

"Business meeting?" Jesse asked, though his body seemed to relax a little.

"Connor is a contractor. Amy's husband recommended him to help me with my riding school. I'm looking to possibly hire him to help me redesign the stables, build a riding barn, and construct an office."

Jesse's lips turned up. "You're really doing it, huh?"

"I'm trying to." She waved her hand toward the window where Connor was pacing outside while talking on his phone.

"I didn't mean to interrupt. I just wanted to say that I was sorry for running off this morning without saying goodbye to you first. But you looked so content sleeping, I didn't want to disturb you. Did you get the flowers I sent you?"

"I did." She picked up the coffee mug and cradled it in her hands, enjoying the heat of it warming her palms. It was a nice contrast to the fall air outside. She didn't meet his eyes as she said, "It was a little weird, though, to wake up and you were gone. No note or anything."

"I…" Jesse rubbed his face. "Oh hell. I'm always messing up with you. I—"

Oscar came up to the table then. "I'm ready to go," he announced.

Jesse sighed but gave his son a short nod. He stood up from the table and said to her, "I'll call you later, okay?"

She nodded, though she still wouldn't look at him. "I'd like that."

"Good." And then in front of everyone in the café, Jesse leaned down and cupped her cheek, forcing her to meet his gaze. Her eyes widened as he closed the distance between them, his lips pressing possessively against hers before he repeated like a promise against her mouth, "I'll call you later."

He left before she could say anything else. Carly's gaze trailed after him, her heart pounding hard. Oscar stared after his father before he looked back at Carly. With a smirk, he lifted his fist and nodded toward it. When she copied his movement, he fist-bumped her, then followed his father out the door.

Carly lifted her hand and touched her lips. Whispers were racing through the café like flames in a brushfire.

Francine came up to her, her eyes twinkling. "Can I refill your coffee?"

"Yes, please." She pushed the cup over to the woman just as Connor returned.

After the waitress left, he asked, "Is everything okay?"

Carly glanced out the window in time to see Jesse and Oscar drive by. Jesse tipped his hat at her as he went.

She couldn't fight the smile on her face as she replied. "Yeah, everything is great."

Chapter Eighteen

Carly had set up a couple of barrels in the corral behind the barn. Even though rodeo was second nature to her at this point, she still wanted to make sure to get in some more practice before the rodeo that weekend. The air was thick with the scent of dust and leather, the steady pound of Nieve's hooves matching the pulse beating loudly inside Carly's ears. She felt the familiar surge of adrenaline as she leaned into the last barrel, Nieve's powerful body moving with hers like it always did. For those fleeting moments, there was no confusion, no distraction. Only the sense of freedom and control she always got when she was on a horse.

Remi and Amy sat on the fence, watching her move. Amy held a stopwatch as Carly and Nieve worked their way through the course.

"Not too bad," Amy said when she finished the last turn.

"Not too bad?" Carly countered. "What do you mean, not too bad?"

Remi glanced at the watch in Amy's hand. "It's not the quickest you've ever done, but it's still impressive."

"Awesome," Carly replied dryly. Even though it was fall, they were experiencing a warm front expected to last until Sunday. Sweat dribbled down her spine as she hopped off her horse. They'd been at it for hours now.

"Why don't you take a break?" Remi said. "I feel like I haven't had a chance to speak with you ladies in weeks."

"That's what happens when you have a double wedding," Amy teased. "You get preoccupied. Besides, I don't have much to report other than Josephine pooping on Josh the other day. While the look of horror on his face was hilarious, I don't have any video evidence to share."

"Well, I don't have much to report either," Remi said. "The plans for the wedding are going smoothly now that Tiffany's agreed to remove me from all decisions for the floral arrangements. Things are getting ordered, and everything seems to be on schedule."

Both her cousin and her sister looked at Carly as she slow walked Nieve around the corral. She rolled her eyes.

"You two aren't very subtle." She tried to bite back a smile though. Carly had been so preoccupied lately between getting the school ready, settling into her new place, and Jesse that she hadn't spent as much time with her family as she wanted to. They were the main reason she moved to Tenacity after all, and she was grateful that they were with her now, helping her with her practices.

"We're old married hags at this point," Remi said. "We need to live vicariously through you."

"You are neither old nor, in your case—" she looked pointedly at Remi "—married."

"Yeah, yeah," Amy said. "Spill the beans. What's going on between you and Jesse? According to town gossip, you and Connor Adair were having an intimate breakfast at the Silver Spur and Jesse showed up with a puffed-out chest before practically having sex with you on the table."

"I never would have guessed that he was the strong alpha type who claims his woman," Remi murmured thoughtfully. "I like it."

"You and those romance novels of yours," Amy muttered.

Carly shook her head. "That's not what happened at all. It was a business meeting with Connor. He's going to do some work on this place so I can get my riding school up and running. Jesse and his son were having breakfast there, and before Jesse left, he kissed me goodbye."

"So you've finally reached the stage where you're kissing each other in public?" Remi said.

"I don't know what stage you want to call it, but yes, things seem to be progressing in the right direction."

"How was the sex?" Remi asked. "You are having sex, right?"

"Remi! You can't just ask people that," Amy said before she turned to Carly. "But feel free to answer anyway."

Carly blushed. "We only slept together once, but…it's the best I've ever had."

"Nice," Remi replied.

"But then afterward, he hid in the bathroom for ten minutes."

Remi winced. "Oh no. What did you do?"

"I…pretended to be asleep when he finally came out."

"Oi," Amy muttered. "You two need to work on your communication skills."

"Well…" Carly smiled a little. "He sent me flowers in the morning, and we talked when we ran into each other at the café. He said he hasn't felt this way in a long time."

"Aww," Remi said, dramatically putting her hand over her heart. "Then you told him you want to marry him and have his babies so you can raise the next batch of rodeo stars, right?"

"I think maybe we should date a few more days before having that conversation," she said dryly.

"But what did you say in response?" Amy asked, getting the conversation back on track.

"I didn't," Carly replied. "His son came up to us, and they left."

Remi tilted her head. "What would you have said if you hadn't been interrupted?"

Nieve nudged Carly as they walked, and she patted his nose. "I don't know. Probably that I'm crazy about him too."

"We're talking love here, then," Remi said.

Carly almost stopped walking, but she knew she needed to cool Nieve down. "I…"

"It's okay, you know," Amy told her. "You're allowed to be loved."

"I know," Carly said weakly.

"And he's a good guy. Stable. Someone who cares about you for *you* and not what fame you bring to the relationship."

"I know," Carly repeated, more firmly this time. The last thing she needed was to rehash her relationship with Fletch. She had to strain her mind just to picture his face anymore. When she tried to imagine the features she'd once known as well as her own, they wavered into Jesse's face, causing her heart to skip a beat.

Amy grinned at her. "Good. So…between Jesse and your plans to move forward with building your school, it sounds like you're not going back on the rodeo anytime soon."

"Nope, I already called Dex and told him to turn down the tour."

"Yay!" Remi said, clapping her hands together. "I was low-key going to be so sad if you weren't there for my wedding. Or worse, if you missed my bachelorette party." She gave Carly a mock glare, her grin tugging at the corners of her mouth. "Do you know how tragic it would've been to drink cheap champagne without you there to make fun of me when I inevitably got sick?"

Carly snickered. "Glad to see you have your priorities in line. You wouldn't have even noticed I wasn't there after the second glass."

Remi gasped in mock offense. "Of course I would have noticed. Who would hold my hair back when I got sick later that night? Amy? I think not."

"Hey!" Amy said.

"Sorry," Remi responded, not meaning it in the slightest. Her expression softened though as she looked at Carly. "But seriously, I'm glad you're coming. It wouldn't feel right without you there."

Carly's smile lingered, warm and a little wistful. "Wouldn't miss it for the world."

The women got caught up a little more before her family finally headed out. After she finished caring for Nieve, she was in the process of returning her gear to the tack room when her phone rang.

She glanced down at the caller ID and sighed before answering it. "Hello, Dex."

"Carly, I want you to hear me out," Dex said in response. "There is more interest in Europe than I think either of us realized. The organizers are begging. They doubled their last offer and said you'd only have to commit for six months instead of a full year."

Carly put the saddle on its rack, her body moving on autopilot. She'd be the highest-paid rodeo star in the world with the amount of money they were talking about. She could almost picture it—standing under the Eiffel Tower, lying on a beach in Portugal, the roar of the crowd, her name echoing through the arena. For years, that had symbolized freedom and security. But it also came with everyone wanting a piece of her and the endless pace of life on the road.

As she stood in the middle of her stable, she realized that she could breathe for the first time in forever, that she wasn't bone-weary exhausted anymore. She didn't want the noise and the paparazzi again. Tenacity, her family, and Jesse and Oscar were all that she wanted.

She looked through the room's window at the paddock she'd worked hard at repairing. She could hear the soft, contented whinnying of Nieve coming from his stall in the other room. He seemed to be as happy with their break as she was.

She had two choices to make: Get back to doing what she did best. Or follow her dreams. She knew what she should do, but the idea of returning to the circuit made her feel like she was trapped in a tiny box that she'd never escape from.

"Dex, look. I know this is an amazing deal, and I'm truly honored they want me to be the headliner that bad—"

"I feel like you're about to say no, and before you do, I also want to make sure you know that the CEO said you could use his private plane to go home whenever you want."

Carly scoffed at that. "It's Europe, Dex. How often do you think I can get home?"

She heard a noise behind her and swung around. Jesse stood a few feet away looking like someone had punched him in the stomach.

"I'll call you back," she told her agent, disconnecting the call even though he'd started speaking to her again. "Hi."

Jesse's eyes were shadowed, his jaw tight. For a moment, she thought he might actually turn and leave without saying a word. Her stomach dropped. All the things she'd wanted to tell him—how she wasn't choosing the circuit, how she'd already chosen this life, chosen *him*—suddenly tangled on her tongue.

But he didn't leave. "You're going to be a headliner in Europe?"

Her phone rang again, and she turned it off.

"I was offered the opportunity," she said carefully.

"I see." Jesse looked pale. "I should go."

"Wait! Don't go! I mean...did you stop by for a reason?"

He was half-turned away, so she could only see his profile. "I wanted to revisit our earlier conversation at the café. It didn't feel like we were finished. But I should have called."

"You can come over here anytime."

"Even when you're in Europe?"

Carly walked carefully over to Jesse. "I didn't say I accepted the offer."

He finally met her gaze. "Why wouldn't you? It sounds like an amazing opportunity. You'd be the headliner."

She tentatively reached out, her hand settling on his taut stomach. "There's a lot of reasons why I should say yes. But there are three reasons why I won't."

Jesse went still. "And what are they?"

"One, I want to open my riding school. I already have things in the works, and I want to see it through. Two, I'm tired of that life. I want to stay in Tenacity and see my niece grow up and my cousin get married. I can't do that if I'm constantly away."

He turned so that he was facing her fully. "What's the third reason?"

"Well…you see, there's this guy that I'm crazy about—"

She didn't say anything more because Jesse had swooped down and captured her mouth with his. Carly threw her arms around his neck, holding him close. Their breathing became uneven as he guided them back into the tack room and over to the counter that was opposite the window.

He hitched her onto it and only then broke their kiss. His hands moved to her ankles, and he removed one of her boots and then the other.

"Don't make this decision based on me," he murmured as his palms glided up her legs to the button of her jeans.

"Did you not hear me mention points one and two? You were third on the decision scale."

"Funny," he said, even as his eyes darkened with desire.

When he went to undo the button fastening her jeans, her hands went on top of his to stop him.

"Promise that you'll wake me before leaving the next time you sleep over."

A smile tugged on his mouth. "I promise. Even if I have to jump on the bed to wake you up. You're a sound sleeper. And you have the cutest snore."

"I do not snore!" Carly replied, affronted by the accusation.

"Sure." His hands started to work on her jeans' button again.

"I'm sweaty and smell like horse," she warned.

He bent his head and licked a strip along her neckline, and she moaned. Her head flew back to give him better access.

"You taste amazing," he murmured against her ear, causing tingles to shoot across her skin. "And you smell incredible. I'm addicted to you. Let me prove it."

Her hands moved to the countertop, clasping it tight. She lifted slightly so he could remove her jeans and underwear. This was home to her now. Not the hotels, not the crowds...this beautiful man before her. Not taking his eyes from hers, Jesse got down onto his knees and pulled her hips toward his waiting mouth.

And then he showed her *exactly* what he meant.

Chapter Nineteen

Carly unloaded Nieve into the waiting stable the day of the Dinosaur Days Rodeo. She had a couple of hours before she was expected to perform, and she was supposed to meet Jesse and Oscar beforehand, but she felt uneasy about leaving her prized stallion unattended.

"Hey, Carly." Remi's fiancé, Shane Corey, walked up to her. Beside him was a tall, handsome Black man who shared a lot of the same facial features. "Have you met my brother, Ellis?"

"I haven't." She turned to Ellis. "But I've met your fiancée, Tiffany, a couple of times before," she said, shaking Ellis's hand.

Ellis smiled. "She does make an impression."

"She does indeed." Carly laughed. "She also makes the most beautiful flower arrangements I've ever seen. Is she here?"

Shane pointed toward the exit of the indoor arena. "Remi's helping her sell flowers."

"Oh..." She looked in the direction he indicated before glancing back at Nieve.

"He'll be safe here," Ellis assured her. "Shane and I are volunteer security. No one's going to be messing with the horses under our watch."

"Yeah, Nieve's in good hands," Shane added. "Remi made me promise."

Carly relaxed before giving Nieve a kiss goodbye on his forehead. "I'll be back soon, my sweet boy, and then we'll put on a show." She turned back to the brothers. "Thank you."

"Go have some fun," Shane said.

She waved goodbye and headed outside. She blinked as her eyes adjusted to the sunlight. The town had gone all out with its dinosaur theme. There were stands selling dinosaur toys and fake bones. A food truck sold dinosaur-shaped cookies. In the distance, she could see people sumo wrestling in inflatable dino costumes. The streetlights had been turned into crepe-paper trees with cardboard cutouts of large eyes peering out.

A gunshot went off, and she whipped around with her hand over her heart. She heard a loud cheer go through the air, and she craned her head in time to see pairs of people rolling hay bales down a track, clearly racing each other.

Once she realized that was where the noise had come from and that she wasn't in any danger, Carly walked toward where she was supposed to be meeting Jesse and Oscar. People waved to her as she went, and she recognized a few of them in return. It hit Carly in that moment that in the few months that she'd lived in Tenacity, it had become home to her.

"Carly," a familiar voice called out. She swung around. Joy sent her hurrying toward the group approaching: Amy and Josh, who was pushing Josephine in her stroller, and, to her surprise, her parents.

She threw her arms around her mother and father. "I didn't know you were coming to Tenacity."

“We missed you girls,” her mom said.

“Plus, your sister told us you were participating in the rodeo today,” her dad added. “You know we’d never miss a chance to watch you girls perform.”

She beamed at both of them, taking in her dad’s weathered face, the new strands of gray in her mom’s hair. She really needed to make more of an effort to see her family—all her family.

“I’m glad you’re here,” Carly said. “I’ve missed you too.”

“During our last phone conversation you had mentioned a boy you were dating,” her mom reminded her. “We’d love to meet him.”

Carly’s lips quirked. “He’s thirty-eight, Mom. Hardly a boy.”

Her mom waved that away. “You’re all kids to me.”

“I hope we get to meet him while we’re here,” her dad said. “I’ve been planning what I want to say to him. After all, it’s every father’s right to give a boy his daughter is dating ‘The Talk.’”

Josh winced. “Maybe you should hold off on that, Arthur. I still have nightmares about the one you gave me.”

Amy cocked her head. “Do tell.”

Josh shook his head adamantly.

Arthur folded his large, muscled arms over his chest. “I made him promise to treat you right…or else.”

“It was the ‘or else’ that gave me nightmares,” Josh muttered. “Especially when he went into detail about how he’d cut off—”

“Just doing my fatherly duty,” their dad said.

“Well, I promise you that you can meet Jesse and his

son later," Carly told her parents. "Actually… I'm supposed to meet up with them now."

"Go on, then," her mom said. "We're staying at Amy's for the week, so we'll have plenty of time to catch up and meet your fella."

"I'll see you later," she promised. She hurried through the crowd and continued on her way to town hall. She spotted Oscar first, standing on one of the steps wearing his noise-canceling headphones. As a large man in front of her moved aside, she finally saw Jesse.

He looked better than ever in a blue-and-gray flannel, jeans that looked made for him, and his trusty cowboy hat.

"Hi, you two!" she said as she ran up to them.

"Hi yourself!" Jesse said. He bent down and gave her a sweet kiss on the lips. Someone gagged, and they pulled apart to see Oscar looking at them with a fake disgusted look on his face.

"Gross," he said. "I don't want to see my dad making out."

"Get used to it, kid," Jesse replied.

He wrapped an arm around Carly's waist, and they started to head to the center of the festival. A couple of teens around Oscar's age came up to them.

"Hey, Oscar," one of the guys said.

"Hi," he replied, practically glowing. He looked at his dad and Carly. "This is Jace and Kevin. They're on the team. Guys, this is my dad and his girlfriend—"

"Carly Hawkins," the one introduced as Jace said. He grinned at her. "Oscar told us about you and your world records. It's cool you're doing Tenacity's rodeo."

"Thank you. I'm glad to do it." Carly felt Jesse's arm stiffen around her, but when she looked at him, he was staring at the teens. Perhaps he was being overly worried again about his son.

"Some of the guys are about to sumo wrestle," Kevin told Oscar. "You want to go watch?"

"Oh, I don't—" Jesse started to say, and Oscar immediately started to tense.

Carly squeezed Jesse's arm. "That sounds like an amazing time. Oscar, you have your phone on you, right?"

"Yes," he replied before looking hopefully at his dad.

Jesse let out a breath through his nose. "Fine. But make sure you're in the arena for Carly's show."

"We'll be there," Jace told them. "None of us want to miss that."

Jesse clasped Oscar on the shoulder. "You'd better get going, then. You don't want to miss your friends wrestling."

Oscar beamed. He and the other two headed over to where a couple of boys were putting on the inflatable dinosaur costumes.

"You did a good thing, you know," Carly told Jesse as he eyed Oscar laughing with the other boys.

He gave Carly a sheepish smile. "I don't know if I've ever seen him this happy. I owe that to you."

Carly shook her head. "You owe it to yourself. You do an amazing job with him."

"Thank you." He caressed her cheek in his hand before giving her another kiss, soft and gentle but both still managing to reach her soul.

They continued to walk through town, taking in the different sights. At one point, she saw Michelle Corey standing in front of a large bouncy house. Above the play station was a banner that read *Sponsored by Little Cow-*

pokes Daycare Center. Carly waved at Michelle, and the other woman waved back.

"I want to speak with Michelle really quick," Carly told Jesse.

"Sure," he replied.

They walked hand in hand as they made their way over to the woman.

"Hi, Michelle," Carly said, giving her a brief hug. "Everything looks amazing!"

"It does," Michelle replied. "I wish I could take credit, but a lot of people put in the work to make this day happen."

Her eyes settled on a good-looking man who stood on the other side of the lot, texting on his phone, his eyebrows scrunching together.

Michelle sighed before turning her attention back to Carly and Jesse. "Are you ready for the rodeo? I keep hearing people talk about it whenever they walk by or drop off their kids."

"I am," Carly affirmed. "Nieve and I have been practicing all week."

"You'll do great," Michelle replied as a little girl with blond curls and a tear-stained face came up to them.

"Ms. Michelle," the girl said, pulling on the skirt she wore. "Bobby Joe threw a sucker in my hair."

She turned around, and sure enough, there was a glop of hair stuck to a red wet sucker.

"That kid," Michelle muttered. "We'll get this fixed," she assured the little one.

"We'll let you get to it," Carly said. "I just wanted to stop by and thank you for getting me involved in the festivities."

"You're welcome. I can't wait to see you perform!" Michelle replied. She gripped the girl's shoulder and guided her to the tall man she'd been eying earlier. He looked up from his phone as they came to a stop in front of him. Michelle said something and he nodded. Carly didn't miss the way the man's eyes followed Michelle as she took the girl inside the daycare center.

Jesse and Carly continued on their way, eventually stopping for a mug of hot cider. Carly noticed that Jesse kept glancing over at the sumo area where Oscar could be seen clapping and laughing with the rest of the boys.

"Do I need to apologize for overstepping?" she asked. "About Oscar."

Jesse laughed, though it wasn't a happy sound. "You never overstep. I told you that before. You know what Oscar needs. Sometimes better than I do."

"Hey." She put her hand on his arm. "You know Oscar better than anyone, and you're an amazing dad. I think I just relate to him. I felt like an outsider for so long when I was a kid, and it was hard for me to fit in. That was until I met Suzie and Arthur. Speaking of, they're in town to spend time with Amy and me. They want to meet you."

"Oh?" Jesse smirked. "We're at the *meet the parents* stage, huh?"

Carly giggled before asking somewhat nervously, "Is that okay?"

Jesse took her now empty paper cup and threw it into the trash along with his. When he turned back to her, Carly's eyes widened at the intent on his face. Before she knew it, Jesse pulled her to him and was kissing her with a fierceness that took her breath away. She wrapped her arms around him, pulling him even closer.

"You know there are children around here," a man said, and they pulled apart only to find Grayson and JenniLynn staring at them with amusement.

"Don't you have something else to do than bug me?" Jesse muttered.

"Hey, bro, you're the one sucking poor Carly's face off like a vampire," Grayson replied.

"Stop teasing them," JenniLynn replied, patting Grayson lightly on the chest. He grabbed her hand and kissed her knuckles. She grinned at him, then turned back to Carly and Jesse. "Carly, they're getting ready to start the rodeo."

Carly glanced down at her watch and swore. How had the time gone by so quickly? She rose up and kissed Jesse on the cheek.

"See you there?" she asked, only to find he had that look on his face again. Like something had upset him. They'd have to talk about it later because she was late.

"I'll be cheering you on from the stands," he told her.

She grinned at him before making a mad dash back to the arena, even as it hurt to leave Jesse behind.

So, this was what it was like to be truly in love with someone.

Chapter Twenty

Jesse watched Carly go, unable to tear his eyes from the retreating figure.

Grayson snorted. "I think you have a little drool on your face."

JenniLynn smiled. "They're clearly in the honeymoon stage."

Grayson lifted an eyebrow at that. "And we're not?"

JenniLynn looked like she was about to show him that they indeed were when someone called out. "Afternoon, Mayor."

She waved to the greeter before urging the men to walk. "Come on."

Grayson took her hand, and the three of them headed to the arena.

"Where are the girls today?" Jesse asked.

"My parents are in town," JenniLynn replied. "They volunteered to take the kids around the festivities so that Grayson and I could have a date."

Jesse clutched his hand over his heart. "And you're letting me be your third wheel? I'm touched."

"Not exactly," Grayson joked. "We thought Oscar would be with you."

"He's with his friends." Jesse nodded to a group of

teenaged boys walking ahead of them toward the arena, clearly done with the dinosaur sumo wrestling so they could watch the rodeo.

"Wow," Grayson said when he noticed his nephew included in the group. "This is a big day. For both of you."

"It's the Carly effect," Jesse replied. "She's good for him."

Grayson nudged his arm. "I'd say she's good for both of you."

Jesse smiled, not trying to deny it. In the distance, a gunshot went off, and JenniLynn scowled.

"They better have those hay-bale races done by the time the rodeo starts," she said. "Last thing we need is for something to startle the horses. Excuse me for a minute."

She left the brothers and headed for the nearby track where the races were taking place. They watched as she spoke to a tall man in overalls who nodded before going into the fenced-in area where the races were taking place.

JenniLynn came back in a huff. Grayson reached up and pushed a strand of her hair away from her cheek.

"Everything okay?" he asked.

"Yes, Al said they just started the final race. Next year, they can move the event to the other side of town. That starter gun is fraying my last nerve."

Grayson pulled her against his side and murmured against her temple, "I love it when you get all mayoral."

"Oh, you," she replied, her cheeks turning red.

"Can you save that for when you're at home? My poor eyes," Jesse deadpanned.

Grayson reached out with his free arm and pulled his brother to his other side. "It's good to have you here, little brother. What are the chances we can get Jonathan, Amanda, Benjamin, and Evie to move to Tenacity?"

Jesse chuckled. "The whole clan? I think you have a better shot of moonwalking on the actual moon."

There was no way they'd get all of their siblings to move to Tenacity. Especially their youngest sister, Evie.

They entered the arena and found seating on the indoor steel bleachers that put them at the center of the course. Jesse would be able to see every move that Carly made. Oscar and his friends took seats in the front row of the same section, to Jesse's relief. He was growing more and more okay with giving Oscar the space he needed, but Jesse was the first to admit that he needed to let go in baby steps.

As he took in the setup, his stomach started to swirl and his hands tightened where they rested on his knees.

"You okay?" Grayson asked.

"Yeah… I just want Carly's event to be done and for her to be in front of me safe and sound."

He didn't have to go into detail; his brother understood.

Grayson clasped the back of Jesse's neck and gave it a light squeeze. "She'll be fine. She's a professional, one of the best in the world."

"I know," Jesse replied, though that knowledge did little to comfort his nerves.

"Mind if we sit next to you?" a woman asked.

Jesse looked over to see Carly's sister Amy with her husband, Josh Aventura. Remi and her fiancé and an older couple were behind them.

"You're welcome to it," Jesse said, waving at the empty spot next to him.

Amy sat beside him. She had her baby with her, sporting noise-canceling headphones similar to what Oscar wore. The kid looked at Jesse with the biggest eyes he'd ever seen.

"She's a cute kid," he told Amy. He had the urge to make a good impression on his girlfriend's family. He wanted—no, needed—them to like him. But…he wasn't lying to be polite. The baby's face looked like it belonged on a baby-food bottle.

"Thanks," she said before turning to the older couple that took the seats in front of Amy. "Mom and Dad, this is Jesse Abernathy."

The older man turned around with a serious expression. From what Oscar had told him when he first started spewing statistics about Carly's family, Arthur was once a rodeo star himself. It showed in his beefy frame. If he was twenty years younger, he probably could have crushed Jesse with one hand. … Maybe ten years younger, Jesse thought as the man shook his hand. The grip was like a vice.

"You're the one dating my daughter," Arthur said, his voice tough.

Jesse didn't flinch. "Yes, sir, I am."

"And you're treating her with the absolute respect she deserves?" Arthur asked.

Jesse tried to keep his face as angelic as possible considering the ways he'd gleefully defiled this man's daughter. He must not have done a good enough job because Arthur's hand tightened enough to make him wince.

"Oh, stop," the woman next to him said. "You seem to forget what it was like to be young and in love."

In love?

Hope bloomed inside Jesse so hard he couldn't even feel the hard grip his hand was in anymore. Had Carly told her family that she was in love with him?

Arthur finally dropped his hand so that he could kiss

his wife on the top of her head. "I haven't forgotten what it's like to be in love. Trust me on that."

"Ew," Amy said. "Can we not?"

The older woman blew out an annoyed breath. "What am I going to do with you two?" She turned to Jesse and said, "Hello, I'm Suzie Hawkins. Nice to meet you."

"Nice to meet you too, ma'am," Jesse replied before looking back at his brother. "This is my brother, Grayson, and his girlfriend, JenniLynn Garrett, the mayor of Tenacity."

They exchanged greetings before Suzie turned her full attention back on him. "And don't let Arthur scare you." Jesse nodded, feeling like he had an ally in Suzie. That was until she said, "He's a softie compared to me when someone hurts my children."

Her gaze turned steely for the briefest of seconds before she turned further around to look at Amy. "Now, let me hold my grandbaby."

Amy laughed before handing Josephine to her mom. Jesse looked blankly at the center of the arena, unsure what the heck just happened.

Amy lightly elbowed him. "Relax. They like you."

"How can you tell?" Jesse muttered out of the corner of his mouth.

"Because despite their tough act, you didn't flinch. They respect that. Especially since we Hawkinses can be a handful."

"You don't say." Josh snickered next to his wife. Amy turned to him with a mock glare, to which he quickly responded, "Kidding. I'm just kidding."

The rodeo started with some amateurs from town. As they performed, a buzz was going through the crowd.

Jesse noticed that more than one head kept turning in their direction.

Josh leaned backward so that he could speak to Jesse behind Amy's back. "You get used to it."

"What?" he replied.

"This tends to happen when more Hawkins family members are together. Especially when Suzie and her mom, Hattie, are in the house. Suzie and Hattie are living legends in this field."

"I see," Jesse replied.

"Carly's technically the last of us to retire," Amy said.

"Is she retired though?" Jesse said, looking around the crowd, taking in the awe on people's faces as they looked their way. He had a sinking feeling in his stomach. He knew that Carly had been offered that deal in Europe. Between the admiration and the money, why would anyone want to walk away from this life?

As though reading his thoughts, Amy said, "There's more to life than all of this." She waved her hand toward the arena.

"Such as?" he asked.

She looked at him like he was a fool. "Everything."

She didn't say anything else, but she didn't have to as she grabbed Josh's hand and pulled it into her lap. He gave her a look that was so tender, Jesse had to look away. He wished that Carly was sitting beside him right now so he could tell her that a life in Tenacity was worth it. A life with him. He'd make sure of it.

The event went on for another hour before the announcer said, "And now, ladies and gentlemen, the moment that you've all been waiting for. Carly Hawwwwkinnnns."

The crowd went crazy as Carly and Nieve came flying out of the tunnel heading toward one of the barrels at breakneck speed. She'd changed into a white shirt with fringe on it and red riding pants that matched her hat. Her face was determined as she and Nieve sped through their routine. Jesse's heart was in his throat as she rode. She was absolutely breathtaking. She was also going so fast Nieve's feet were a blur.

"She hasn't lost her touch," Amy said beside him.

"Go, Carly!" her dad shouted.

"I wonder if she's about to break another world record," JenniLynn murmured beside him.

Before he could respond, Carly headed toward the final barrel. But as she went sharply around the corner, a gunshot rang out through the air. Nieve jerked at the unexpected noise and stumbled to the ground, taking Carly with him.

"No!" Jesse yelled as the large beast landed on top of her.

He jumped to his feet and ran down the steps as fast as his legs would go. He was somewhat aware that Grayson and Carly's family followed him.

"Dad," Oscar called out as he hurried over to him. "Is she okay?"

Jesse couldn't answer. He hopped over the barrier separating the bleachers from the dirt floor of the arena. By the time he reached Carly, the event medic was there along with a wrangler who pulled Nieve off to the side, where a vet was inspecting him closely.

"Carly," Jesse whispered as he finally reached her. He came to an abrupt halt as he stared at her. She lay there, not moving. He watched as blood dripped from her mouth.

The air thickened in Jesse's lungs until he could barely breathe. For just a second, Carly's body blurred and he was staring at the lifeless body of MaryBeth. She was dead. Carly was dead, and he hadn't even told her how much he loved her.

Arthur and Suzie hurried by him, the older man limping as he went. Suzie dropped to her knees.

"Sweetheart," she murmured, carefully holding her daughter's hand.

The medic waved smelling salts under Carly's nose, and she came to with a groan.

"Darlin', you scared the life out of us," Arthur said.

"Wha-what happened?" she whispered. She sounded feeble, not anything like the strong woman he knew.

JenniLynn came up to them, looking angrier than Jesse had ever seen her.

"One of the men from the hay-bale races dropped the starting pistol they'd been using, and it went off," JenniLynn explained quietly. "I'm so sorry. This will *not* happen again."

Jesse barely heard her over the buzzing in his ears, causing everything to sound muffled.

"We need to get her to the hospital to be looked over," the medic said.

"Will she be all right?" Suzie asked.

"I'd wager she has a concussion and possible fractured ribs, but they'll be able to examine her further there."

"Nieve…" Carly murmured, her eyes unfocused.

"We'll make sure he's looked after," Amy said.

Carly's gaze finally landed on Jesse. She gave him a weak smile he couldn't return. He felt like he'd turned to stone.

"We're going with you," Suzie said.

Carly looked at Jesse one more time before she closed her eyes. Had she passed out again?

"We need to get her there now," the medic urged.

Shane Corey was waving an ambulance in through the large entryway at the side of the arena. Two EMTs loaded Carly onto a stretcher and pushed her quickly toward the waiting vehicle.

"Dad?"

Jesse turned his head, dazed. Oscar stood next to him, his hands clenching and unclenching by his sides.

"I..." Jesse didn't know what to do. His head felt like it was made of cotton. The noises around him became muffled.

"We've got you, champ," Grayson said. He and Jenni-Lynn quickly escorted Oscar out of the arena, but not before giving his brother a concerned look.

The only thing that registered in Jesse's muddled brain was that Oscar was safe.

He turned back in time to see them load Carly into the back of the ambulance.

It was just like before, when he watched them load MaryBeth into one. They'd closed the door on him then too, blocking the last view he'd had of her alive.

He'd lost the love of his life that day. Never in a million years did he ever think that he'd be lucky enough to find a love that great again.

But he had.

And history was repeating itself. As the ambulance lights lit up and took Carly away from him, all Jesse could do was stand there and stare.

Chapter Twenty-One

Carly was supposed to be resting. Instead, she was staring out of her living room window, hurt and anger warring inside her. She was on day three of recovering from a concussion, sprained wrist, and overall bruising that happened when a thousand-pound horse landed on you. Thankfully, Nieve had rolled off her quicker than he fell, but she was left feeling like a punching bag.

She could deal with that. She'd had worse falls before. What she could not deal with was Jesse Abernathy going silent on her. Again!

He'd texted her a few times to make sure she was okay, but she hadn't spoken to him or seen the man. Considering the direction she thought their relationship was going, she figured he would have at least visited her in the hospital when they'd kept her overnight or that he would have stopped by her house since.

But nothing.

She'd tried calling him a few times, but she always got redirected to voicemail.

Carly tried to be understanding. She had a vague memory of Oscar being there when she'd gotten injured. He'd been upset, and Jesse would have had to calm him down before he overstimulated.

That was three days ago though.

"Honey, you should be lying down," her mom said.

Between her parents, Remi, and Amy, Carly should have been fine with not seeing Jesse. They'd made sure she lacked for nothing from company to food. But as much as she loved her family, they weren't the ones she needed to see right now. She needed to see her boyfriend and give him a piece of her mind.

Tomorrow. The doctor said you can drive tomorrow.

"I'm fine," Carly insisted. She turned to face her mom and sister who were currently visiting her. "I'm seriously okay. I love and appreciate you both so much. But I think what I need is some alone time. I'm not in any danger at this point, and it'll be good for me to have a second to think."

Amy's eyebrow raised. "And what are you thinking about?"

Carly let out a sigh. She turned to face the window again, staring sightlessly at the woods bordering her property. "I'm thinking I should have taken up Dex on his proposal and hightailed it back to the circuit."

She could see Amy and her mom exchange glances in the window's reflection.

"You're reconsidering?" Amy asked cautiously.

Carly briefly closed her eyes. As much as she wanted to say yes, she knew there was no way she was going to leave Tenacity anytime soon. She wasn't a quitter, and she wanted to see her dream come true. She was also going to chew out Jesse and tell him that he needed to choose. Her and better communication skills, or nothing at all.

Because Carly was done with him going AWOL and giving her the silent treatment.

"No," Carly finally answered. "I'm not leaving Tenacity. If this recent injury has taught me anything, it's that I'm getting too old to be doing this."

"You're thirty." Her mom said it lightly, but there was relief in her voice. "You're hardly over the hill."

Carly shook her head. "I know, but my life goals aren't the same anymore. I want to start my horse-riding school, Suzie-Q's Healing Hooves."

She'd decided to use her dad's nickname for their mom as a way to honor both her parents. Her mom instantly teared up, recognizing it.

"Oh, darlin'." Her mom came over and hugged Carly carefully. "You girls spoil me."

"I don't think any of us are going to top that one though," Amy said before jokingly adding, "Way to show us up, sis."

"You can always name your next kid after Mom," Carly returned.

Amy snorted. "I'll keep that in mind."

Their mom turned to look at Amy, her eyebrows raised. "Do you have something to tell me?"

Amy rolled her eyes. "I'm not pregnant, if that's what you're asking. I'd like Josephine to get a little bigger before we try for baby number two."

"Anyway, thank you for keeping me company today…" Carly said, hoping her family would take the hint.

"Okay, we'll get out of your hair," her mom replied. "But you call us if you're feeling uncomfortable or need anything at all."

"I will. Thank you both for everything."

She smiled as she watched them go, but the little joy

that their presence had sparked inside her dimmed as she went back to staring out the window.

Rodeo accidents weren't going to be the death of her.

But Jesse Abernathy very well might be.

There was a knock on the door, and for half a second, she thought it might have been her family returning because they forgot something. A quick glance around showed that nothing was amiss though—no items left behind.

And then, against her better judgment, Carly started to feel hope. Maybe it was Jesse finally coming to check on her. She was back to debating if she wanted to throw herself at him or tell him to take a hike.

Another knock vibrated the door, this one even more insistent than the last. Carly hurried down the hall but paused in front of the hallway mirror to give her hair a quick check. She wouldn't win any beauty contests at the moment—not with the dark circles under her eyes and the pallor to her skin—but she'd do.

Taking a deep breath, Carly opened the door.

Her jaw dropped at the sight of the man before her.

"Hello, beautiful," he said with his thick Aussie accent.

"Fletch."

Jesse manually sanded the board of his front porch. He needed something to do with his hands.

He couldn't think. Couldn't focus.

He ached to see Carly. He felt more and more gutted the longer he stayed away.

As much as he wanted to see her, though, he couldn't get the image of her lying lifeless on the arena floor. His mind kept playing that moment relentlessly on repeat until he couldn't breathe.

Jesse needed to sort out his brain before he saw her, or he might just end up begging her to never get on her horse again—a conversation that he knew wouldn't do either of them any good. Knowing how strong-headed Carly was, she'd probably slam the door in his face if he tried—her resilience was one of the things he loved most about her.

No, he needed to get his crap together before he went out of his mind from not seeing her or touching her to make sure she was alive and well.

A car pulled up to the house, and he looked up in confusion when he saw who it was.

"Hi," Amy Hawkins said when she got out of the car. "The house is looking good. I always thought this was too pretty a piece of property to not have some life on it."

Jesse ran down the steps to her. "Is Carly okay? Tell me she's okay."

He bit back bile. Why else would Carly's sister be here other than to tell him that Carly's injuries were worse than originally thought?

"She's fine," Amy assured him. "Well, as fine as can be expected. The doctor said she should be able to start driving tomorrow. She's champing at the bit to do so. I know she's got a lot of things to get in order before she leaves town again." She walked over to the side of the house, admiring the boards. "Are you going to paint this? Because I have to tell you, it looks great natural."

Jesse barely heard her over the ringing in his ears. "What the hell do you mean that she's leaving town?"

"Oh!" Amy looked at him, surprise on her face. "Didn't she tell you? I thought you two had grown close. When

I stopped by to check in on her this morning—because that's what people do when they love someone—she had mentioned something about calling her agent and accepting the European tour."

Jesse dropped the hammer that he was still holding. It barely missed his foot. He didn't even notice. He was too busy staring at Amy with horrified eyes.

"She can't leave," he whispered.

Amy shrugged. "What does she have in Tenacity worth staying for? Last week I would have said you. Just going by town gossip and what my sister has told me, I thought you'd end up like Josh and me. I've never seen Carly as happy as she's been with you, but I've been over to her house every day since she was injured, and I haven't seen you there, Jesse."

"I… I had things I needed to do."

"Well, I hope they were important." Amy walked back to her car and opened the door. She nodded toward the house again. "It really is shaping into a nice home. I'm sure you and your son will be very happy here for years."

Jesse didn't miss the fact that Amy hadn't included Carly in that statement.

He stood frozen as he watched her drive off until she was gone from view, then he slowly turned and went inside the house to grab his car keys and wallet.

Once he was in his truck, he pointed the vehicle toward the only direction he ever wanted to go again.

Chapter Twenty-Two

"What are you doing here, Fletch?" Carly couldn't believe her eyes as she gripped the door handle so hard it almost injured her good hand.

Her stomach twisted sickeningly at the sight of the man who'd once turned her life into tabloid fodder. The open door allowed a cool fall wind to surround her, and somehow that made the moment feel heavier, like a ghost from her past had suddenly shown up to run its fingers down her spine. She shivered in horror. It had been almost a year since she saw the man last. Frankly, she would have been fine never seeing him again.

"I missed you," he replied. He took a step toward her as though he'd planned to kiss her.

She moved quickly away, turning to go deeper into the house. "You missed me? I haven't seen or spoken to you once in months, but you missed me?"

She could still see as clear as day the time she walked into the stable that his dad owned. Fletch had asked her to stay on the circuit for another year, despite the homesickness she'd been experiencing since Elizabeth left Australia, and she'd sought him out to discuss it more. She hadn't wanted to say yes, but he said that he could get them on the cover of *Outback Sports Magazine*—one of the biggest in the country. The sponsorship deals that came with doing a cover of such a prestigious magazine would have paid her double what she'd been making. And that had almost been enough to convince her to stay. Because in the back of her mind was a space full of childhood trauma—of things being taken away and smelly secondhand clothes being thrown at her and the uncertainty of whether she'd get to eat that day.

She'd convinced herself that staying was the right thing to do. She could move back to the States the next year after she got more money. But as she'd rounded the corner to tell Fletch, she'd found him naked, rolling around in a fresh hay bed with some groupie. She'd yelled at him, told him that they were through. She didn't know why it had been that breaking point for her. It wasn't like he was ever faithful to her, and she knew it. She guessed knowing and seeing it in the flesh were two different things.

A few days later, she was injured when her friend's horse had startled, and Carly had found herself headed home shortly thereafter.

Fletch looked at her now, giving her an angelic look that did nothing for her. "You disappeared on me," he said, "and blocked my number. How was I supposed to tell you how I felt?"

Carly crossed her arms, being as careful as possible not to aggravate her injuries. "You seriously can't think that I would have wanted to speak to you after what I saw that day. Besides, you and I both know that you don't feel anything for me. All I've ever been was a publicity tool for you and your daddy's rodeo circuit."

"We were good together."

"No." She eyed the man in front of her. He was tall

and muscular with long blond hair that fell to his shoulders and eyes the color of the ocean. At one time she been taken in by his attractiveness. She knew better now that the blinders were off. What she once had thought was confidence she now knew was arrogance. He was the type of guy who *knew* how good looking he was. He used that and his father's money to his every advantage.

He narrowed his eyes. "What do you mean no?"

"I mean what I said. You and I weren't good together, nor were we in love with one another. We had an incredible run that gave us enough publicity to help people know our names, but that was it."

"Is this because of that guy you were seen dancing with?"

Carly stilled. "What are you talking about?"

Fletch grabbed his phone out of his pocket and pulled up an image. It was grainy, but she recognized it right away. The picture was her and Jesse slow dancing at the Tenacity Social Club the night of the fundraiser. She had a vague memory of someone taking her picture, but she hadn't thought too much about it because she'd been so intoxicated with Jesse.

She stared at it now, seeing that and several others of them were all over the tabloid's website. Even now, in Tenacity, she couldn't escape them. She felt violated. And worse, she'd brought Jesse into it. That was all they needed—for the press to descend when Oscar had just started to adjust to school. She could only hope that it would blow over. It wasn't like she was Tom Brady or someone of that caliber. People in the States didn't follow rodeo like other countries did.

But…how was she going to explain all of this to Jesse,

in case the press did show up? She fought back the urge to cry.

"I have to admit," Fletch said, "the press in Australia is not being too kind to you right now. They're saying you're flighty."

Carly looked at him in absolute disgust as her anger started building inside her. "Let me get this straight. It's well known that you cheated on me with multiple groupies—"

"You know that was all alleged."

She ignored his remark. She knew what she'd seen in that hay bed. "And I move on with the man of my dreams, and I'm the flighty one?"

"Man of your dreams?" Fletch's face twisted, and he didn't look so handsome in that moment. He laughed dismissively. "I doubt that."

"I'm in love with him," Carly replied more firmly, even though she fully planned on giving Jesse a piece of her mind the next time she saw him. "I have every intention of spending the rest of my life with him."

Fletch ran an impatient hand through his hair, his face full of disbelief. "You're kidding me."

She raised her chin proudly. "I'm not."

Fletch began to pace. "You and I aren't built like that, and you know it. That's why we were so good together. I *know* you, Carly. You love the lights and people shouting your name. You're addicted to the fame, just like I am."

Carly was done with this conversation. She started walking back toward the door. "You don't know me at all. I never loved the invasiveness of the press, the complete lack of privacy. I liked the money. I won't deny that. But there are more important things to me now. Rodeo isn't everything."

Just like her mom said all those weeks ago.

Fletch stiffened. "What are you saying? You're going to throw away your career on some hick from Montana?"

"He's not a hick," she said, whirling back to face him. Jesse was a man with integrity who fought for those he loved. He had grit and a heart of gold. He was everything she ever wanted and more.

"You can't seriously be settling in some backwater place like Tenacity." Fletch ran a frustrated hand through his hair. "You're Carly Hawkins—rodeo-circuit darling. That life is in your blood. You can't give up the career you love for this guy."

"You're not hearing me, which just proves some things never change," she said, her chin lifting stubbornly. "There's something else I love a lot more now—*someone* else."

"But what about the European deal?"

Carly stiffened, and Fletch's eyes went wide, as though realizing that he'd slipped for the first time in his life and made a mistake.

"How do you know about that?" she asked before she realized the truth. "You're behind it, aren't you? You and your dad's entertainment company?"

Fletch met her eyes. "Dad's letting me head up the tour in Europe as long as you sign on."

Carly looked down at the floor, feeling stupid. They hadn't wanted her for her. They'd wanted her because Carly Hawkins and Fletch Alistair made headlines, and their messy relationship sold seats. "Your dad's business interests will survive without me."

"But I won't!" Fletch replied insistently. He gave her an imploring look. "After you left the Australian tour, sales dropped by forty percent. The only reason we've gotten any interest in Europe is because of rumors that you'd be a part of it. You know that together we'll be unstoppable. I need you to be a part of this."

Carly felt dirty. This had always been the heart of their relationship. Fletch never gave a damn about what her thoughts and needs were. He only cared about what she could do for him.

She continued to the front door and started to open it. "The answer is no."

"You're being ridiculous," Fletch said, his face turning ugly as he started to lose his temper.

"I know this is going to come as a surprise to you, but for the first time in your life, someone is telling you no. You're going to have to deal with that." She opened the door fully but kept her eyes on Fletch. "I want you to leave, and don't ever come back here again. We're done."

"Carly—" he started to say.

Another voice interrupted him. "You heard the lady."

Carly swung around to see Jesse standing on her porch. Her emotions practically flew out of her chest at the sight of him—anger, relief that he was there, guilt over those pictures, worry about what he would say. But most of all, the all-consuming love that she felt for this man.

Jesse had on his cowboy hat, shadowing his eyes. It gave him a mysterious, menacing air. He gave her a brief once-over to make sure she wasn't in any danger before he turned his attention back to Fletch, giving him a look that made Carly nervous.

"I believe she asked you to leave," Jesse said. He didn't raise his voice, but he didn't have to. The calm authority in his tone was enough to make even a man like Fletch flinch.

She had never seen Jesse this way. There was a quiet danger to him. Moreover, there was a protectiveness in the way he angled his body toward her. She hadn't felt this safe with someone since the first day she'd met her parents and they'd promised her that nothing would ever hurt her again. She hadn't realized she needed that sense of protection still—until Jesse gave it to her without a word. Something healed in her at the steely-eyed look in Jesse's gaze as he stared Fletch down.

"The lady and I are having a private conversation," Fletch said, all bluster.

"The conversation is over," Jesse said, his voice low in a way that enthralled her.

The way he was acting shouldn't have turned her on, but it did. Her pulse leapt deliciously at the way his eyes narrowed on Fletch. Honestly, she needed to stop listening to Remi go on about those romance novels of hers. It was making Carly think ridiculous things. But she couldn't help it.

She really hoped they weren't about to get into a fight. Not in the middle of her hallway anyway. While it would have been satisfying to watch Fletch get knocked down a few pegs, she didn't want him to actually get hurt. He was such a baby when he was.

"Go on, Fletch," she said. "Leave."

Fletch looked from Jesse to her. It was clear that he was internally debating: Did he try to argue with her some more, or did he realize that Jesse could very well knock him on his butt if he didn't do as he was told?

"What a disappointment you are," Fletch spat before he headed toward the door. Jesse took a step toward him that made Fletch recoil, but Carly held up her hand to stop him from going after her ex.

“The feeling is entirely mutual,” she replied.

Fletch walked by Jesse, giving him as much space as he could given the width of the porch. Jesse watched him go, not taking his eyes off the other man until the Aussie was in his rental car and heading down her driveway. Only then did he turn back to Carly.

Carly leaned against the front door, her earlier hurt and betrayal at his absence after her injury quickly rising. “You have a damn nerve—”

Jesse stepped into the house and grasped her shoulders, slowly backing her up against the wall. He then cupped her cheeks in his palms and lowered his head, kissing her as if his life depended on it.

Chapter Twenty-Three

For just a minute, Carly gave in to the kiss before she pushed against his chest. He broke away from her only to stare at her with fiery torture in his eyes.

"Carly—" he started to say, but she walked away, back into the living room.

She heard the front door close and then his footsteps as he followed behind her. When she turned around to face him, he was reaching out as if to grab her again. She took a step back.

"Don't," she said so coldly that he reared back a little. She wrapped her arms around her waist, hugging herself.

She loved this silly, foolish man so much. But after today, she might never see him again. Well…that was impossible in a town as small as Tenacity. They'd see each other again whether they wanted to or not. And it'd be like a knife stabbing her every time she did.

"I deserve that," he muttered.

He looked so broken that she had to turn away. She went to her favorite spot in front of the large living room window and stared at the paddock and woods in the distance.

"Who was that guy?" he asked.

"My ex. And he's not what I want to talk about right

now." She couldn't bear to look at Jesse. "It's been three days of near complete silence from you. Is it because I stepped in when Oscar asked to hang out with his friends at the festival? I thought we'd made peace with that. If you don't want to be with me anymore—"

"Stop," Jesse interrupted. She could see in the reflection that he took his hat off and tossed it onto the nearby chair. "For once in my life, I can't blame my actions on being an overprotective dad..."

She turned to face him then, leaning her back against the cool window. "What do you mean?"

Jesse ran an aggravated hand through his hair. "The way I've been acting had nothing to do with Oscar. Probably since the first time I saw you, I've been afraid. And when I saw Nieve fall onto you, it brought all my fears to the surface. I saw you lying there, and I couldn't even think. Oscar was starting to panic, and Grayson and JenniLynn had to step in and help him. I was paralyzed. I couldn't have done anything if I wanted to."

"But why?" Carly said, trying not to cry. "Why do you keep pushing me away? What are you afraid of?"

"Losing you," he confessed in a pained whisper. "I can't lose you."

The anger and hurt that had been pulverizing Carly since he pretty much went no contact, relented as she heard the anguish in his voice. "I don't understand. I'm right here. I'm not the one pushing anyone away."

"I know," Jesse replied, taking a careful step toward her. "But when I saw you lying there, it reminded me of the day I found MaryBeth."

The remaining rigidness left Carly. In all the scenarios she'd come up with to explain his behavior, for some silly reason, this was one she hadn't thought of. It seemed so obvious now.

Carly walked over to the couch and sat down. She looked at him and then the spot next to her. He took that as the correct cue and took a seat beside her.

When he didn't say anything, she said softly, "Tell me about it."

"I'd come home from my job. I'd been employed at this company working in IT doing analytical work. I hated it. MaryBeth and I had been fighting more and more about it. We lived in the city, and it was suffocating me. I'm a country boy through and through, and I thought Oscar might benefit from the fresh air instead of the city pollution. MaryBeth didn't want to move. All the best schools for Oscar are in Houston, she'd say.

"The night before she died, we had gotten into a really bad fight. The kind where I ended up sleeping on the couch. We were polite to each other the next morning, but there was tension like I'd never felt before in our marriage. We really loved each other, but that last year, we seemed to be on completely different pages. I hated how we'd left things that morning, and I'd felt uneasy that entire day.

"By the time I got home, I was exhausted. All I wanted was to eat dinner with my family, put Oscar to bed, and then talk to MaryBeth and see if we could come up with a compromise. Instead, I came home to Oscar screaming his head off, saying, 'Mommy won't wake up.' I found MaryBeth in the kitchen unconscious."

He turned his head and briefly wiped at his face. She reached out and grabbed the hand that was closest to her.

He looked down at it blankly before continuing with his story. "I watched them load her up into the ambulance.

I couldn't go with them, not with Oscar as hysterical as he was. Thankfully, my brother Jonathan was in Texas, but he was still an hour away. By the time I was finally able to get to the hospital, she was gone."

He reached across from her and picked up her injured hand. He leaned down and kissed the brace covering her pulse before he gently placed it back down.

"I blamed myself for years," he admitted. "If I hadn't stressed her out maybe she wouldn't have—"

"No, don't." Carly started peppering his face with kisses. "Don't do that to yourself."

He half smiled at that. "The damage is already done, I'm afraid." He leaned his forehead against hers briefly before pulling back again. "I felt like I owed it to Mary-Beth to be the parent she was to Oscar. I said it before, but she was amazing with him. I put all my efforts into taking care of him. We stayed in Houston for years, in her dream house. I had no time for anyone else other than the occasional fling. I didn't want to find the time. It was safer that way, you know?"

She nodded. She did know. She'd spent a good chunk of her life pushing people away because it was easier than risking her heart on them.

Jesse tucked a strand of Carly's hair behind her ear. "Then you came along, and here we are."

Carly held his hand to her cheek. "And where is that?"

"I love you, Carly," Jesse said. He didn't even hesitate. His voice became urgent as he begged, "Please don't leave me."

"I'm not going to," she assured him. How could she? He was her cowboy. He and Oscar were her family now. A party of three.

"But—" Jesse gave her a frustrated look. "I know, okay?"

Carly frowned. Maybe she was distracted by his confession of his feelings, but she somehow lost track of their conversation. "Know what?"

Jesse's hand fell to her waist as if holding her there. "I know that you're going to accept the European tour. If it's what you really want, I won't stand in your way, but I don't think it is. I think you want your school and me and Oscar. And I—"

She put a hand over his mouth to silence him. "Who said anything about the European tour?"

He kissed her palm before moving it away from his lips so he could answer. "Amy stopped by my house a little while ago. She told me."

Carly huffed. "That busybody." She gently grabbed Jesse's chin. "I want you to look into my eyes when I tell you this for the last time. I'm not going on the tour. I'm retiring from the circuit to focus on my school."

Jesse's forehead furrowed adorably. "Then why did Amy—"

"—tell you otherwise? If I had to guess, she was playing Cupid and got tired of us pussyfooting around each other."

Jesse looked at her hesitantly. "You said it was an amazing opportunity though. I don't want you to give it up because of anything holding you back here."

Carly shook her head. "I'm doing this for myself. The rodeo lifestyle isn't what I want anymore. Besides, I found out today that my ex was behind the tour."

"Is that why he was here?" Jesse asked.

Carly sighed, remembering that while she could promise Jesse until she was blue in the face that she'd never leave him, it didn't mean he wouldn't want to leave her after what she had to say…and she couldn't blame him.

Jesse took her good hand and held it against his leg, like an anchor keeping her steady in turbulent seas.

"Tell me about it," he said, echoing her earlier words and she smiled sadly.

"Elizabeth and I were making a name for ourselves in Australia. We were traveling all over, getting sponsorship deals right and left. The truth is I've always had this unhealthy drive to be successful in everything I do. I was consumed by it, needing to make sure that no matter where I went in the world, I'd never have to struggle again like I did when I was a child."

She told him this without meeting his eyes. It was her dirty secret, how much she desired success, to never go without money again.

"That's understandable given everything you went through as a kid."

She shrugged a shoulder. She appreciated him saying so. "And then the unthinkable happened. Elizabeth's husband died unexpectedly, leaving her a single mom. She lost all her zeal for life and the circuit, and she decided it was time for her and the kids to go back to the States. She told me I should come with her, but around that time, I met this bull rider, Fletch Alistair. He was your typical spoiled rich boy who only got top billing in the circuit because his father owned it. He wanted credibility, and what better way to do that than to date one of the Hawkins Sisters?"

Carly's mouth pursed with bitterness as she recalled how hard he pursued her.

"Fletch made sure that they scheduled our events on the same day so that we'd always run in to each other. If sponsors came in to see him because of his direct connections to his dad, he'd make sure to introduce me, always wrapping an arm around my waist. Pretty soon, we were taking pictures together, and people assumed we were dating. When I joked one day to him about how people thought we were a couple, he very seriously told me that we were. I accepted it. He was fun when times were good—a nice distraction from my increasing homesickness—but he was never anything serious to me. However, the public *did* take us serious. Pretty soon, we were being followed by paparazzi wherever we went, and they'd scream the vilest things. About me and my childhood. Nothing was sacred. When I'd ask Fletch to use his connections to get them to back off, he looked at me like I was crazy. He said, 'There's no such thing as bad publicity, Car!'

"I started to feel like I was living in a nightmare. On top of the tabloids digging into my past, Fletch's relations with groupies who followed the circuit was getting back to me. He told me to stop being jealous when I'd ask him about it. I wasn't jealous—I was humiliated. I finally told him I wanted to go home. He told me about a deal that would make me even wealthier than I was at that point. I almost agreed to stay for another year, but I walked in on him with someone."

Carly gave a sad shrug.

"The rest you know. I came back to the States. What I didn't know was that without me and the Hawkins name, Fletch has been struggling. He said seats aren't selling out anymore. He's behind the offer I was given for the

European tour. He wanted a repeat of our notoriety. I told him no."

"You're giving up rodeo?" Jesse asked. He seemed to be holding his breath as he waited for her answer.

"I told my agent the other week that I was done. I want to focus on my school. The Dinosaur Days Rodeo was my last performance."

Jesse looked like he was doing his best not to smile. He carefully wrapped his arms around her. "Soo…is there anything else you want beside your school?"

"Subtle," she joked before she grazed his lips with her own. "You, duh. Because I love you too."

"Thank God," Jesse muttered before he pulled her to him again.

When they finally broke apart, Carly asked, "What does all this mean? For us?"

Jesse brushed his thumb across her lips as though he couldn't stop touching her. "I can't walk away from you. I love you too much. I know it's a lot to ask, settling down with a guy who comes with a teenage boy who has autism."

She frowned. "You know I care very deeply for Oscar. How could I not? He's a part of you. Which is why I should warn you…someone took pictures of us at the Tenacity Social Club."

"I know."

Her eyes flew to his. "What do you mean, you know?"

"Oscar's a sports junkie, remember. He follows all the news. He told me about it a couple of weeks ago."

"What…why didn't you tell me?"

Jesse gave her a confused look. "I figured you were used to that kind of thing. It didn't seem a big deal."

"And you're okay with it? Being splashed in the tabloids like that?"

"I wasn't thrilled, but I would never leave you because of it."

"What if they show up here and start causing issues for you and Oscar?"

"Oscar's got a whole football team that's willing to protect him now, thanks in large part to you."

Carly tried not to smile at that. "And what about you? Would you be okay if the press showed up here and started taking your picture?"

"As long as I get to keep you, I'll ask them to get my good side and go about my day."

She let out a laugh, unable to believe how well he was taking this.

"Did we solve all of our issues for the day?" Jesse asked.

Carly didn't try to hide her relieved grin then. "For now."

"Good."

He tugged her carefully onto his lap and captured her mouth in a kiss, his tongue sliding against hers. The kiss deepened, his arms wrapping around her, pulling her against him until not even air separated them.

When they pulled away to draw in an erratic breath, he said, "You want to know what this means for us? I can't do casual. I don't need to see where this goes. I know exactly where I want this to end. With you and me in a church before all our friends and family. I want to marry you someday. Hopefully, someday soon. This isn't a proposal, mind you. I'm going to ask you properly after I've put some thought into it. I want it to be a proposal to remember."

Carly felt the same sincerity she read on Jesse's face. "In that case, I think you should know that when you ask me, I plan to say yes."

She shifted on his lap and almost moaned as she settled more firmly on his obvious need for her. She pushed down, and he sucked in a hard breath at the movement.

"It's too bad I don't have my house completed yet," Jesse muttered as he rocked up into her. "I don't even have a place to offer you."

Carly stilled. "I guess it's a good thing I have plenty of room here for you and Oscar."

Jesse seemed to get momentarily pulled from his haze as he registered her words. "You'd be okay with us moving in here someday?"

"Sure," Carly said. "After you make an honest woman of me. Can't have the town gossiping about me that way."

Jesse snorted. "Of course. I guess one of my siblings can have the house I've been working on—"

He stopped talking as Carly began to trail kisses on his neck.

"Sounds like a plan," she said after giving his skin a final nibble. "You should probably ask me to marry you soon, then, so we can figure out the living situation that much faster."

She reached between them with her good hand so that she could palm him through his jeans.

Jesse swore under his breath. "It's too bad you're injured because I really want to make love to you right now."

Carly giggled, feeling carefree for the first time in what seemed forever.

She climbed off Jesse's lap but held her hand out to him. When he looked at her questioningly, she said, "This ain't my first rodeo."

He burst out laughing. Getting up from the couch, Jesse swung Carly into his arms, and they headed to her room.

* * * * *